I0676799

The
Street President

By

Alonzo Roberts

Library of Congress Control Number: In publication data

Copyright: © 2015 by Cash Talks Publishing Group

ISBN 13: 978-0-578-16038-2

Cover Design: Mario Patterson

Edited by: Sherrill Woodruff

Author: Alonzo Roberts

Published by: Cash Talks Publishing Group

ACKNOWLEDGMENTS

I want to thank God for blessing me with many talents and for keeping me in his arms throughout my journey.

I would like to thank my brother, Daymien "Dutch" Roberts for always being sucker free while being lockdown for thirteen years+. They don't make em' like you no more.

Shout to all the real people that's locked down in this prison system

A special shout out to my kids; Chardanay Harris, Tiera Lloyd, Alonzo Roberts aka A.J, Jada Roberts, Yanique Boreland, and Zion Roberts

A shout to my sisters; Syretta Roberts and Denisha Roberts

Shout out to my brothers; Jab Roberts and Dashawn"Murder" Roberts

Jab, I love you and thanks for going through all the chaos in the streets with me; you never turned your back on me.

Devon Johnson, you been more to me than a good friend you're my brother. I appreciate you.

To my Uncle Brian Roberts; thanks for being an Uncle and Father at the same damn time.

I want to give a shout out and respect to Bernard Cornish aka Pooh John and the Alive and Free movement.

Shout outs:

Raheem Spencer, D.J Gee Q, Illstrip, TracShac, and all of those who supported the CashTalks Records Movement, Blackboy, Dutty-General, Jon Aka J.Hall, Skillz, Jammers, Jeff Palmer and his beautiful wife Latasha Ellerbe-Palmer, Jeff Archie, Lexx, Smurf, Big Mike, Tymaine Coleman, Lil Joe, Fatboy, Face Manhattan, Chris "Heatroc, Ellerbe, Tyzek Roberts, Alecia Roberts, Ziare Roberts, Tyren Roberts, Tryniti Lake, Raevyn Williams, Dashawn aka D.C, Whiteboy Chuck, MMG thanks for the support, Ninth Street Book Shop. Everybody that's left on 27th Street that ain't FRAUDIN', Free Mike Benson! Free Murder! R.I.P Wellz, and Jack, R.I.P Pearl Higgins 2-4-57 to 12-20-08 I miss you, Aunt Pearl. R.I.P Aaron Clifton.

A special thanks to Krystal Thornton for believing in me and supporting team CTPG.

Oh yeah, I almost forgot y'all-HATERS!!! Y'all been hatin' on me for a long damn time. I want to acknowledge you for the great job you do of keeping my name relevant. My accountant loves y'all keep doing what you do!

A special thanks to my business partner, Ms. Reid, at Cash Talks Publishing Group, LLC. Thanks for being there for me, not just sometimes all the time. Thanks to you, C.T.P.G

Dedication

Claudette "Dutchess" Roberts
AKA
"QUEEN"

CHAPTER ONE

North Side 1995

Pumpkin slid her plump lips from my throbbing tool and said, "I think I hear somebody comin'…" I peered through the cracked door to see if Queen or one of my sisters was in the cut trying to be nosey. The hallway was empty. I took hold of my mans and stroked him a bit before easing it back in her mouth. She hesitated; I palmed the back of her head forcing her to take in all ten inches filling her mouth. "We good, ain't nobody here but me and you." She continued making love to me with her talented tongue. My mind was at ease as I received my weekly stress reliever. I was only thirteen with responsibilities of a grown ass man; it was only right to indulge in the pleasures of one as well.

I leaned up against the door just in case the *Get along Gang* happened to appear. I loved my family to death but my Mom loved to be in the midst of straight action; my sisters Mish and Bree were no better. Pumpkin had been topping me off on the regular for the last few months on the D.L. She was a booster, seven years my senior that stayed over in King Plaza with her two small children. Queen brought clothes for my little sister and brother from her. She always had the fly shit from the GAP, and the high end stores in King of Prussia. Despite her profession she pretty much kept to herself. She was an alright looking light skin jawn with an okay body. Her ass wasn't phat to death, her tittes weren't big, but her mouth was wide like a Sea Bass with thick soft lips. A lot of dudes slept on her because of what she lacked in looks. I on the other hand had a gift to see deeper and seek out talent. Ms. Pumpkin definitely had a hidden talent.

I grabbed the back of her head holding it steady as I worked my tool in and out of her mouth rapidly. "*Ugh*-Oh shit I'm bout to bust," I warned her. Her grip around my dick tightened. I placed both of my hands around her head while my young seed slid down her throat. Once I was done unloading, she swallowed it. I don't know why but that made my dick harden every time she did it. The other broads would spit it out or jerk their head away fucking up my nut. I should have expected that. They were young girls who ain't know nothing about pleasing a man. I put my mans back in my boxers and turned on the light. Pumpkin was getting up from her knees. She was quiet and her eyes stayed glued to the floor the entire time. Normally she would crack jokes. Today something was not the same.

"You alright, Pumpkin?"

She brushed passed me and grabbed the door knob. I took her hand off the the knob and grabbed her arm gently.

"Yo, what's up with you?" I asked again.

She looked up at me with tears in her eyes.

"Am I ugly to you?" her voiced cracked.

"Huh? No-not at all. You already know that type of stuff don't matter to me. I like you, you're my friend." I stroked the side of her face. To be my age I had an effect on the females. My charisma was on point. I got it from my bitch ass daddy.

"Then why don't you touch me?"

"What are you talking about, I do touch you," I knew where she was going at with this. I knew it would come up sooner than later. I made the mistake of showing her too *much* attention lately. I needed a stash spot because Queens's dude, Roy had been stealing from me. I couldn't prove it, but it was a no brainer. No one in the house besides him had a history of getting high. After school, I been going over to her crib to chill and knock off a few sales. No one knew I was fucking with her; I wouldn't have an issue with no one trying to run up in her shit.

"Babe, I told you I was a virgin. I'm saving myself until I am mature enough to handle a real relationship with a real woman like you. I'm only in the 8th grade and I got school, my family and these streets to worry about. I can't let you get me pussy whipped. I already get side tracked by your bomb ass head," I lifted her chin; she closed her eyes as I placed a soft kiss on her awaiting lips. Her body quivered and her lips parted. I pulled back quickly. She traced her tongue slowly over her lips, "Be patient, and when the time is right it will happen. Your baby dad will be home from his bid in a minute and you won't be thinking about my young ass." I cracked a smile. A small smile appeared on her face. I pulled her close and wrapped her body in my arms, "You're cool peoples, Pumpkin." I kissed her cheek and opened the door. I watched her as she walked down the hall to the steps. When the front door opened then shut. I heard a burst of laughter and my closet door swung open.

"Am I ugly? Why don't you touch me..."Mish, my twelve year old sister mocked Pumpkin. She was hiding in the closet the whole time.

"Yo, you wack! You was in my closet the whole time?" I picked up the half-filled 2 liter bottle of *Tahitian Treat* that was on my dresser and threw it hitting her in the thigh.

"I'm telling Queen that you had a grown woman sucking your little Wee-Wee! And I'm telling her you hit me!" she snapped holding her thigh.

"I don't care tell her, I'ma tell her you was in my closet watching, *nasty!*" I retorted.

"I'ma tell your dumb girlfriend, Amber that you not only letting, Pumpkin suck your wiener, but you be doing it to all those other girls-watch." She stuck out her tongue and bolted out the door.

I didn't have a come back for that one. Mish, was a real bitch and didn't give a fuck about nothing else but *money*. I couldn't afford to let her tell my baby about the shit I was doing on the side. I loved Amber, but the broads loved me. I was stuck between a rock and a hard place like my grandma used to say. I opened my top drawer moved my socks to the side took a stack of money folded in rubber bands out. I peeled of five one hundred dollar bills and ran after my sister. "Yo Camisha, let me rap to you for a minute." She was half way down the steps with the phone in her hand before she whipped around to face me.

"What boy, I'm about to make this phone call," she smirked. I started down the steps. A smile spread across her face when she saw what was in my hands. She pushed her designer specs on top her nose and placed her hand on her hip.

"Didn't you want a pair of those pink field timbs that just came out?" She snatched the money and threw me the phone.

She tucked the money in her bra and went back up the steps.

The door opened and Queen faltered with grocery bags in hand, my little brother Careem, and sister Cabree trailed behind her. I ran down the steps to take the bags out of her hands. She had not too long ago suffered a bad accident that left her slightly disabled. That is the reason why I had taken over her business. The disks in her back had suffered massive damage. She was in pain most of the time and pretty much had to chill. She damn sure wasn't supposed to be carrying groceries.

"Mom, where Roy at?"

She sighed heavy and shook her head. I know what that meant. He was somewhere getting high.

"I don't know, baby."

She knew where he was at, but I didn't have the energy to get in to it with her. I was the middle child, and the favorite of my mothers', Clara "Queen" Reynolds, six children. We lived in the huge corner house on 27th and Tatnall courtesy of Wilmington's' Section 8 program. We've been here for as long as I can remember. The entire time we lived here my mom has been handling shit on her own. I had no idea why she even fucked with a joker like, Roy. Queen, was the HBIC in all of Wilmington. She supplied just about every hustler on the Northside. She had been hustling since she was my age, my oldest brother Gary, father turned her on to the streets. They were like the black Bonnie and Clyde and got money any which way they could until he met his demise, six months after she gave birth to my brother. The Wilmington PD, ambushed him after they received a false tip that he was the one who raped and killed a sixty year old white woman in Brandywine Hundred. Queen swore somebody in her family set him up. They hated him because Queen was supposed to go to college like the rest of her siblings; not run the streets with some, hoodlum. What they didn't know was that Queen didn't just love Big Gary, she was in love with money and addicted to the thrill of getting it. After the police shot her man down, she found herself alone.

Unwilling to go back to her parents she decided to continue on with the lifestyle of a hustler. She did everything from selling weed, running girls and having her own bootleg after hour establishment. The after hour is where she met my dad, Dorian Fields. He was a major player, a flashy gambling man. The ladies loved him. He stood six foot five inches tall with an athletic build; light skin niggas was the look in his day, however, Dorian was an exception. His smooth dark chocolate skin, wavy hair, and bedroom eyes had broads throwing their panties at him. Queen was no exception; she told us the story of how they met the regret showed on her face. She fell deeply in love with him and he had her under his spell. It didn't matter that she was a headstrong woman when Dorian got a hold of her she was like putty in his hands. They were hot in heavy relationship long enough for her to birth my brother Dutch, me and Camisha. It took years but eventually she grew tired of his cheating ways and unlike big Gary he didn't get money he lost it; his gambling habit had crippled his home.

It was while she was knocked up with Mish that she found her escape; Dorian got locked up for kiting checks. She reluctantly packed up and went back to my grandma's until her section 8 came through. Although Queen was unwilling to fully submit to her parents wishes; she did go back to work in her parents corner store on Vandever Avenue. Pregnant and with three small boys to look after she didn't see no other way to survive; she was not the innocent girl they once knew- the four year University dream was over. She did however enroll in Delaware Tech Community College and took up Early Childhood Education. She lived the life of a square for three years; she obtained her Associates degree and got a job a Wilmington Head Start on Governor Prince Boulevard. She was now living in the house I would know as home, she met another guy and my youngest two siblings were born from the relationship. It was like a cycle with Queen shortly after the kids were born, their father got knocked in the head for armed robbery. The feds scooped him up to serve a thirty year bid.

Big Gary's right hand man, Stacey, had stopped in to check on Little Gary and he took Queen out for dinner. Three days later our life changed for the better. Stacey was a major Hustler in Florida and blessed Queen, by turning her on to his Columbian connect. He knew Queen was a down ass broad, and a hustler. He had seen her put in work in their hay day. He always had feelings for her on the low. A lot of men had wished to have her on their arm; her curvaceous thick body was firm and appetizing. The years of running track and playing on the Howard High School basketball team had done her well. Her brown sugar complexion had a glow her thick long black hair is what broads these days pay a grip to have glued in their head. Her attitude topped it off. She knew she was the shit, yet she was humble. She was about her money, and didn't wait for any man to give it to her. She was the type to go get it with you-a rare breed. In a matter of weeks Queen was supplying the whole city. There were men who weren't too happy about a broad running shit. No one said anything because they knew her reputation. She took shit from no one and no one tried her.

Queen continued her reign until she was in the car accident that nearly took her life a year ago. She had taught us all how to get money, but she took to me. I didn't know why. Maybe it was because I looked so much like my father. She always said I had his ways, but I was also just like her. Little Gary was doing his thing with weed, and Dutch didn't play too much with the drugs, he was more about doing the things the ski mask way. I on the other hand loved money and I wanted to make the most money as possible anyway necessary. Queen saw that and taught me *everything* about the business. After the accident everything was turned over to me and I controlled the streets with her guidance. With any form of power there is responsibility. The question was if I was really ready to endure it.

CHAPTER TWO

Present Day

"Give me $50 on pump 2."

I placed the crisp Grant in his hand and headed out the door. My son, Dorian the III, was already on his job. I was glad, the hawk was out and it wasn't even November yet. I hopped in my toy for the day, a Mercedes R-Class minivan. Today was Queen's birthday and we were having a party for her at *Celebrations* on Market, later that night. I was taking my kids to do a little shopping for their grandmother. I knew in the back of my mind it would end up being a shopping day for them as well. I didn't mind they were all pretty much good children. There was one I had to keep close to me and that was my fifteen year old daughter, Darianna, her mother was the love of my life- Amber. Never in a million years would I have thought Amber would not have had my last name. In her sophomore year of college she cut me off, she could no longer deal with me being in the streets or the infidelity. I had fathered two children on her; my son, I had with Pumpkin, my seventeen year old daughter Ariel, was by a broad I was pantie pushin' with. I didn't find out about her until last year. It's funny how money and fame will bring people out of the wood works. I tried to fight it till the end. There was no way I could have gotten her pregnant when one- I was only eleven when we were humping and two -I never stuck my dick in her. After thousands of dollars on lawyer fees, the child was mine. The DNA don't lie. Last there was my six year old son Prince, by my ex-wife. We were only married for eight months. She was there to pick up the pieces when Amber left me. When I found out she was pregnant I married her. That was stupid-we had nothing in common. So divorce was the plan.

My life was great but damn did I have challenges along the way, but that is what happens when you are a *Boss*. Situations always come at you from every angle, friends, broads, and even your family act weak. I just learned to be proactive and not reactive; reaction is what is getting these niggas bodied on a regular. I handled my life like it was a chess game, I left them checker playin' niggas alone.

****

"How long are you going to be gone?"

Her naked body was stretched across the King sized bed, the red satin sheets complemented her caramel complexion. TaNeka was one of my runners slash playmates. She was thirty-four and a registered nurse at A.I Dupont Children's Hospital. I met her two years ago when Prince was admitted for his asthma. She was over his care and was very attentive to him. I thought she was just doing her job. One day I came without my girl and she let her true colors show. She let me know she knew that I was the infamous Dorian "The President" Reynolds. Her tongue was slicker than oil. She left me no choice but to make her show and prove. She topped me off in the bathroom. It was supposed to be a one-time thing but she wanted more and I never turned down great healthy head; plus she could be of use to me. She had access to prescriptions-particularly narcotics. I took her out to dinner at *Firestones* on the riverfront. I wined and dined her talking that slick shit making her feel like she was special. Then we walked hand in hand along the pathway enjoying the site of the moon reflecting upon the Delaware River. I made sure I had her open before I popped the question. To my surprise she wasn't feeling my proposition. She got a little loud, made a scene and stepped off. I didn't look at it as defeat; I just had to turn to plan D.

I followed her back to the parking lot, apologized and then took her to my *smash pad* out in Appleby Apartments. When we first went in I could tell she was nervous, she scanned the area looking for any traces of a woman. She knew I was married, I told her we were separated and headed for a divorce. I told her to take a seat on the sectional and get comfortable. I poured us both a glass of Rose and took a seat next to her. After a few glasses I had her butt naked bent over the couch taking every bit of my thick massive dick. She was so gone that I had her screaming, *"I'll do whatever you want"* That was what I expected. We been getting money ever since and I've been occasionally giving her the dick just to keep her in check.

"I don't put a time limit on my family," I was in front of the dresser mirror pulling my dreads in a ponytail.

I watched her sulk and throw a silent tantrum. *I need to let this bitch loose.* She was damn near forty and acting worse than my six year old. She already knew what the deal was. Our relationship was business first anything else was a privilege-period.

"Why can't I go? Oh never mind I guess your wife is going to be there," she huffed and rolled her eyes.

"Look, I already told you this was for family and Queens close friend only. What I tell you about bringing that wife shit up, I'm not with her." I stated calmly.

"Then why haven't you fucked me or took me out in six months? I suck your dick, put my job on the line by stealing meds, and you can't even let me meet your mom. This is so fucked up in so many ways, Prez. I love you, I'm putting my life on hold for you. I'm not getting any younger." she started her crying shit. I wasn't going to let her get under my skin. I regretted that I let her stay over here. A few months ago she hit me with a story about her landlord selling his house. I knew it was bullshit, but I let it go. My lease was up here next month any way. I was going to renew it for another year, but her fucked up attitude messed that up.

"Speaking of your job, I thought about it and you're right. I shouldn't have you put your job on the line. I know longer need you're services."

I walked out the room to the coat closet. I heard her feet slap against the floor. I turned around to put on my jacket and she stood in the middle of the living room with her eyes bucked and mouth hanging open. I fastened my Ralph Lauren Peacoat, placed my scarf snug around my neck.

"Prez, wha-what you mean by that?" she said softly. I chuckled on the inside. Her entire attitude changed. I opened the door, as I was walking out I reiterated, "You're dismissed."

****

My toy for the night was a 7 series Ruby Black Metallic BMW, I pulled it off the lot earlier in the week. It was an early birthday present to myself. This was the first time I drove it since the purchase. I turned my iPhone off, and turned on the Blackberry the only calls I was taking tonight was business. My staff already had been instructed not to bother me tonight. All my important calls were directed to Raela, if anything was too much for her to handle then she would ring my phone. The life I lived was hectic. I started out pushing weight in Wilmington for Queen at the age of twelve, by time I was sixteen, and I had my own squad working for me with a reach from Claymont to Seaford. I didn't touch anything. When I was 18, Stacey was impressed by my progress and brought me down to South Beach to turn me on to something greater. He was getting tired and ready to retire. He wanted me to take over his Southern region. I was with it, all I could think about was all the money I was about to bring in.

I remember that day like it was yesterday. We were sitting on the C-Level roof top terrace of the Clevelander Hotel enjoying the beautiful blue-green ocean view, listening to the sounds of the hot D.J and of course watching the fly ass cars coast up and down Ocean drive. The females were on point as well; but getting money came first. I was a firm believer that pussy was a nigga's biggest down fall; it was proven way back in the bible days with Samson and Delilah, you all know the story…

"Good afternoon, gentlemen," a voice as sweet as a sugarplum echoed in my ears. My attention was immediately turned in her direction. Standing before me was a 5'7 brown skin dime piece. She was clad in a flowing Yves Saint Laurent pale yellow sundress. Her long tresses blew delicately in the light winds. Her plump breast fit snug in the low cut-V. Her look was sexy yet eloquent. I felt my dick get hard. I placed the menu on my lap and smiled nervously. She rolled her eyes and slapped the back of my head catching me off guard.

"Boy, I know you ain't acting brand new on me!" she said ghetto girl style.

I was confused. She must have had me mistaken for someone else. What I did know was she better not hit me no damn more. She was heavy handed. I looked at Stacey to check his peoples. They both busted out in laughter. I was getting heated by the moment.

"Yo, what is so funny?" I rubbed my head.

"You really don't remember me, huh? She slid next to me and wrapped her arms around my neck. Her scent reminded me of a passion fruit mix. I couldn't help but notice her plump firm melons that made me want to get lost in them. I could feel the saliva build up in my mouth.

Stacey cleared his throat bringing me back to reality. I shook my head.

"Naw, I don't." I drank the rest of my drink.

"Dorian, it's me-Raela!"

I sat the glass down slowly. I took a good look at her face and I felt like an ass. It was Raela, but I didn't remember her looking like this. She was Stacey's niece; he took care of her while her parents were doing a life bid. Queen used to babysit her when he went out of town. She was like my best female friend. She was always a pretty girl; she was just a little on the heavy side. I had to take up for her a lot, because people would tease her because of her weight. Calling her names like Fatty R-buckle, real cruel shit. She moved away when I was like 11 and I hadn't seen her since. I would always ask Stacey about her but he never really said anything and he didn't say she asked about me, she was out of site out of mind. But I never forgot about her. I pulled her in close to me and hugged her tight. I let my hands explore every curve on the low. Her body felt right and I got harder. We continued our embrace for a minute. My dick was rock hard and poking her in her side. She pulled away blushing. That's the day that our business partnership began. She was the legal side of my operation. She was in school for Public Relations, and studying real estate on the side. Nothing ever transpired between us besides business, there was a couple of times we came close, but decided that it would be foolish to cross the emotional line. She was everything I wanted in a woman, I'm sure if we had reunited under other conditions she would be carrying my last name.

I pulled into the parking spot and noticed my younger sister outside bent over in some niggas Honda. I shook my head. I was not for Bree's shit tonight. I got out the car hit the alarm and popped the trunk to retrieve the gift box. As I was shutting the trunk I got a good glimpse of the outfit she was rocking. She wore a tight red sequin off the shoulder dress. Her Remy parted down the middle with a red glitter head wrapped around her forehead. I stopped myself from laughing she looked like an Indian Christmas Ornament. These broads didn't have a clue to what a real man really wanted. The thing that got me is I know she paid a grip for the outfit, and she didn't look no better than the other Rainbow, Forever 21 shopping broads.

"It's about time you got here!" her tone was nasty.

"Nice to see you too Dorothy, I mean Bree," I teased after taking a look at the shoes. She flipped me the bird, flung her ass length weave and turned her attention back to the young boys in the car.

When I walked through the door, D.J Gee Q was doing his thing on the tables; 2 Chains was blaring through the speakers, screaming all he wanted for his birthday was a big booty ho. Speaking of big booty ho's Misha was on the floor with a few of my cousins getting it in. I knew she had to be wasted. Misha tried to be too cute all the time there was no way she would be on the dance floor wild' in out like she was. I laughed and made a mental note to get all this on video. I always had to have some leverage to keep her ass in in check. Fuck with me I'll have her ass on you tube in a minute. I went up to VIP Queen, Gary, and of course Roy was up there having drinks. I went over to her and kissed her on the cheek. She was looking fly in a tasteful black beaded cocktail dress by Emilio Pucci. Her micro braids were pulled tight in a decorative bun. There was enough ice on her to freeze the entire party. My mother sported her name well tonight. She was a Queen and her children were her royal court.

"It's about time you got here I was starting to worry," she said in a hush tone planting a kiss on the side of my face.

"I had to control a pest. You know how it gets."

She twisted her lips and shook her head. I handed her the box.

"Open it."

A wide smile spread on her face as she shook the box in a childlike way. I couldn't help but grin. I loved seeing my mother happy.

"Is it empty? I don't hear anything and it's awfully light," she inquired.

"Weren't you the one who told me to never judge what something is worth by the package?" I reminded her.

She nodded; pleased that I had taken heed to the many jewels she had dropped through the years. As she started to open the box, I noticed Roy scooting close with his bug eyes fixed on the package. *He won't get his filthy hands on this.* I made sure that he would not be able to steal this gift from Queen like he had done with the many others. The box was finally open and she reached in and picked up a white envelope, she opened it and pulled out its contents.

She held the envelope to her heart and her head dropped. She erupted in emotions as her shoulders moved up and down while tears trickled down her pretty face.

Gary wrapped his arm around her shoulders. He already knew what was in the envelope because he went half on the present. Queen had always talked about traveling out of the country for vacation. The money was never the issue, it was the responsibility she had with us kids and holding down the business. She had come upon the destination while watching a documentary on the traveling channel. Since then she was hooked and said one day she would go. Queen wasn't getting any younger, so Gary and I decided to send her now while she would still be able to enjoy it. We paid for her to attend the Sandance NYE celebration at the Atlantis Palm Hotel in Dubai. She was to leave the day after Christmas and return January third. Her best friend Gail was going with her, of course we paid for it. The best thing about it was Roy was not invited. This would give my brother and I time to get rid of this leech.

"You boys, I-I don't know what to say," She held her arms out and we both gave her hugs.

"You don't need to say nothing. We want you to enjoy yourself, you deserve it." Gary said.

Roy peeped in the box to see if anything else was there.

"What ya get, money?" he asked eagerly.

Queen turned to him. "No there sending me to Dubai," she stated joyfully.

"Du-what? Did you want to go there? Where that at?" he asked with eyes shifting from me to Gary nervously.

"Yes, she wants to go there. If you really knew her you would know that's all she talked about the last ten years," I retorted.

"Oh-Oh now I remember when we leaving?"

"*We* are not going nowhere, she is going with Gail." Gary interjected.

Roy looked to Queen to say something but she was too busy reading the brochure. Roy knew he was outnumbered, he grabbed his drink and stormed out of the VIP. Gary and I slapped hands we knew that nigga was swole. We also knew that he would do anything to fuck up her shit. So I kept hold of the tickets until she was to leave' if he tried to take those he would force my hand to kill him.

I took a seat over at the corner table and poured myself a glass of Remy Martin Louis XIII Champagne Cognac. Gary sat in the seat facing me with a mixed drink in his hand.

"What's going on Izzo?" he asked leaning back in the chair.

"Shit. I'm tired as hell. I been running all day."

"What was up with the pest talk?" he raised an eyebrow and took a swig of his drink.

"Man that ain't about nothing. My house guest in Appleby just got exterminated."

He laughed, "Damn what she do now?"

"Man, she on some dumb shit as usual. She already knew what it was when we hooked up in the first place."

"I told you to stop treating these bitches like they wifey. You buying them jewels, taking them out and letting them live up in your crib you sending mixed signals." He went on and on. "Just let them do their job and be gone. All that personal shit is going to hurt you in the end."

I heard it all before. I did a lot of bullshit but at the end of the day I did have a heart- using and abusing was not my thing. I wasn't a sucker but I was fair. I wanted to see all of my people eat. That's how I got my street name "The Street President." I looked out for my community and those whom I employed. I figured if I kept everyone happy I wouldn't have to worry about people getting hungry and coming at my neck. My method worked for the most part. Of course I had minor situations that occurred but they were handled without anyone getting hurt. Crime was down and I knew that my rule had plenty to do with it.

Gary was still going on about my woman issues. I poured myself another drink. I was going to need one to endure this. I took my drink to the head when I noticed Amber coming in my direction. She was stunning in an Erin Fetherston black laced top flare dress. I grinned at the site of her attire. I had brought that dress for her a few months ago when she her husband and I went away to Vegas. Most people could not understand our relationship. We were all grown and had one thing that connected us-my daughter Darianna. She was the key and for her sake we made everything work.

"Hey honey." She kissed the side of my cheek and sat next to me.

"What's up babe? Where's the hubby?" I joked.

"Down stairs at the bar drinking with Dutch," she looked to Gary and got back up to give him a hug, "Hey brother I didn't notice you over there." She added.

They exchanged pleasantries then he excused himself to give us some privacy. Something was up I could see it in her eyes.

"You good?" I asked.

"Yeah and No…" she waived her hand.

"Which is it, yes or no?"

"Did your daughter tell you that she is suspended for operating a dating ring at school?"

I sat up in my seat, "Yo, run that by me again?"

"Darianna has been running an escort service with her friends. She supposedly had six boys from the football and basketball team pay her $100 dollars apiece to go on a "date" with her friends. She then in turn paid the girls $40 dollars to do the date."

I couldn't believe what I was hearing. I put my head down and my hand up to cover the smile on my face. My baby was about her money just like her dad and grandma. I know Amber was pissed but I was proud in a way. I was upset that she was prostituting broads but damn she was killing them.

"Dorian-Dorian..." she smacked my hand from my face, "I know you not laughing!"

I couldn't wipe the smile away quick enough. She shook her head and swatted me again. "This is not funny, she could catch a charge behind this."

"Naw-Naw babe...You right, I'm not laughing at that I'm just saying-Yo, she crazy," I busted out laughing.

Amber couldn't hold it in she started to laugh too.

"Boy, you need to talk to your child she is doing too much. I let the candy operation go, but now she got these girls "dating" though. Thank God, I'm cool with their parents. You know I'm going to need you to straighten them out with a little something too." She said. I already knew where she was going with it. The parents were most likely pill poppers or needed to get on the list for the toy drive my center held every year. I would look out for them to keep my baby straight.

CHAPTER THREE

The next morning I woke up at my normal time-six o'clock on the dot. It didn't matter what time I went to sleep my body was programed to rise at that set time. I sat up in my Amalfi King platform bed and took a deep breath. Last nights festivities played back in my head. Everything went great; Queen was surrounded by everyone she loved and those who genuinely loved her. Roy of course never showed back up; Queen didn't seem to notice. After I spoke with Amber, I thought about cutting the night short and taking Darianna home early so we could discuss her latest caper. I went to the first floor to retrieve her but she was on the dance floor partying with her siblings. I decided to wait for today to talk with her. She and lil Dorian were the only ones here anyway. Ariel went back home, she claimed she had something to do. She never stayed around much. She was a senior in high school and I knew she needed her privacy. They all were teenagers that's why I purchased this mini mansion in Bohemia Mill Pond, out in Middletown. It had five bedrooms one for me and each one of my kids. I had the mini-van for her and Lil Dorian to share. Darianna was working on her permit. She wasn't with the mini-van look. I tried to explain to her that she could have a car of her own when she could make money of her own. I told them all that.

It's not that I didn't have the money to buy them a car. I instilled my kids with values. They had to work for what they wanted. Getting good grades were a given but I had to see that they were responsible as well. Darriana was a whole other monster. She was so much like me it was scary. Money stayed on her mind at all times. She would get it at all cost which could be a blessing or a curse. I had to get her in check before she got too far off. I sunk my feet in my slippers, stretched and went to the bathroom to freshen up.

I traveled downstairs to my gym and lifted some weights while thinking about how I was going to handle my daughter. In the midst of my work- out I turned on the news. I went to the small fridge to take out the ingredients to make my morning protein shake. As I was pouring everything into the blender; the words breaking news shot across the screen. I turned the blender on and watched the screen. There was a bad fire out in New Castle. I stopped the blender and turned up the television. The broadcaster went on and talked about the three alarm blaze. When the address popped on the screen I wasted no time in running out the house. I raced up Rt. 1 with nothing on but my gym shoes and sweatpants. I didn't stop to get a coat or anything. I couldn't believe my building was on fire. My mind went straight to TaNeka. I couldn't call her because I left the cell phone in the house. The only phone I had on me was my business phone and that was because I left it in the car the night before. I reached Appleby in less than twenty minutes. The aroma of charred items was in the air as soon as I passed the Wal-mart. I parked in Scotch Hills apartments and walked across the street. There were police cars and a few fire trucks, and plenty of news reporters on the scene. I went over to one of the officers and told him I occupied one of the apartments and wanted to know what happened. He directed me to the property manager that was on the scene.

I walked over to the young white man and introduced myself. The property was under new management and I never met with them until now.

"I'm Dorian Reynolds, and I live in building 200 apartment 4." I extended my hand. He took a hold of it and shook it.

"Hi, I'm glad to see you made it out. As you can see there is nothing left except the structure." He pointed to the collapsing building.

"Is everyone ok?"

"I'm still not sure. We have gotten in touch with everyone except three families. We are hoping they weren't in," he looked at my attire oddly.

"I didn't stay here last night. I had-"

He stopped me, "No need to explain. I understand. You're lucky you weren't here. I have to go, but I'm going to need you to contact your insurance and let them know what is going on. We have your number on file and will be back with you first thing Monday. Please be patient with us. I know it must be devastating to lose everything." He walked away. If he only knew- my focus wasn't on material possessions.

I walked around the grounds to see if I could find TaNeka. After walking in circles for about an hour, I called it quits.

I took a seat in the car, retrieved the phone to put in a call to the hospital to make sure she wasn't admitted or worse. I called and there was no record of her which was a good thing. I had been dealing with her for a minute but I didn't know too much about her family. She tried her best to get me to meet her friends but I avoided it at all cost. I wasn't trying to get that deep with her. I hoped she wasn't hurt. I was going to just wait a few days and call her job. I knew she wouldn't let that go.

I rode down rt. 40 to get on route 1. My phone rang. I looked at the phone and Raela's face popped up. She was calling from my other house I had on tuck near Speakman Park, Raela had an office there and occupied it when she was in town for business. I looked at the clock it was just about eight o'clock and it was Sunday. She wasn't due to be in town until Tuesday. I picked up the phone.

"Hey babe," my tone was dry.

"We have a problem…" she stated firmly.

I sighed and pulled the phone away from my ear; took a deep breath and went back to the call.

"What is it?" I huffed.

"Marco was shot and the Apple street location was robbed. Everything is gone." There was dead silence between us for about five minutes. I turned left to get on Rt. 1 headed north. It was ironic that my apartment building caught on fire and my pill spot gets hit in the same night. Something wasn't right.

"Where are you calling me from?" I asked remaining calm.

"I'm on my way back to Apple Street. I went inside the basement. All ten barrels are gone, which means someone knew it was there and had the right vehicle and manpower to move them quickly." She added.

"Give me ten minutes." I hung up the phone and called my brothers. I told Dutch to bring me something to wear. I forgot I was still not dressed. I called lil Dorian and let him know that I wouldn't be back home any time soon. When I arrived in front of the townhouse Gary and

Dutch's vehicles were already parked out front. I pulled up in a vacant house driveway three doors down, I noticed the house had a sold sign in front of it. I ran up to the house and Raela was sitting on the couch fully suited up looking like she was about to attend a board meeting. Dutch was slumped in the chair holding his head, and Gary sat next to Raela stoned faced. He rarely cracked a smile.

Raela looked me up and down and shook her head. "You sure got here fast from Middletown. What you do a buck fifty?"

"Nah, I guess you didn't see the news?" I took a seat across from her.

"No I was pretty much assessing the damage here," she stated sarcastically.

"My apartment out Appleby caught on fire. The entire building burned to the structure." Everybody wore a puzzled look on their face.

Dutch even sat up when he heard that.

"Yo, get the fuck outta here? You serious?" he asked.

"Yeah Dawg, I'm dead serious. I left the babe, Neka in there. I went to see if she was cool. I couldn't find her nowhere out there."

"Did you call the hospital?" Raela inquired.

"Yeah, she ain't there." I said.

Gary kept silent I could see he was in deep thought.

"This has not been a good day for you so far, huh?" she said.

"Naw, it hasn't. What's up with Marco, is he breathing?" I asked.

"Yes he is for the moment. If he can't give me a story that sounds correct he won't be for long." Raela crossed her leg and sat back. "He was shot in the thigh. It just missed a main vessel. He is in surgery as we speak. I had Detective Samuels send one of his men to guard the room…just in case."

"You think he had something to do with it?" Marco had been working with us for the last five years. I didn't think he would rob us, but times were hard in these streets you never knew what a nigga would do.

"I don't think he did it but he was reckless. I found this," Raela held up a Ziploc baggie containing a red pair of thongs. "There was no force entry nothing was broken, however if you go upstairs you will find that the mattress cover is missing. They found him in the back of the BP down the street."

"They kidnapped the nigga?" Dutch said.

"So the bitch set us up!" Gary broke his silence. He shook his head and bit down on his lip.

"Pretty much' that's why I need our friend Marco to tell us who she was. She is the key to finding fifty thousand dollars worth of Percocet.

The number is minute, but it's the principle. If they feel they can hit us once they will do it again. What if that was a major shipment from the pharmacy? What if money..."

Gary cut her off. "Fifty thousand that was about to turn into a quarter of a mill! I want to know who the fuck knew there was even anything in this house. We don't sell shit from here." He snapped.

Raela turned to Dutch.

"I need you to stay here for a while. I have a funny feeling about this. I'm going to have to look for a new place but we have to stay close to the port. I have to go to the office and see what I can buy. I don't want to deal with our outreach homes. The government is on those deals and it wouldn't be a good look."

"Did we fill those yet?" Dutch asked.

"All the houses over Northside are filled. We have one on Union and two on Townsend street- why?" she asked.

"I got this young jawn that I'm feelin' and she need a spot." Dutch said smiling.

"Dutch, man five of your girls already got spots. I can't keep giving houses to your jump offs man." I stated.

"You only got two broads in Delaware houses. The others are spread out; besides, it's not like that, she a good girl she got a job at the nursing home and everything. Her mom on that shit and

she be getting high in front of her son and shit."
He explained.

I took a deep breath and looked at Raela.
She waved her hand signaling to me that she
would take care of it. I swear sometimes I felt like
I was the oldest when it came to Dutch. The only
thing he thought through carefully was a caper,
everything else was a joke. We discussed our
plans for the next hour. I had to run over to
Queens to get an outfit because Dutch didn't do as
I asked. Gary was short on words his brain was
ticking fifty miles a minute.

He was going to find out what was going on.
If this type of thing continued to happen it would
hurt him majorly. He was a foreman down at the
Docks and he was over the shipments that came in
from our overseas pharmacist.

My operation was broken down in four
sectors. Raela and I oversaw everything. We
controlled the real estate development, The
Royalty Youth Foundation, and The Queens
Outreach which was private housing for young
mothers, and struggling families. Like
Wilmington Housing Authority had the section 8
program and projects we owned two 50 occupant
apartment buildings and over 80 scattered sites
through-out Delaware. We have done the same in
the State of Florida, Georgia and North Carolina.
Our headquarters was housed in the Reynold's
Center which was a state of the art youth center

located on the Riverfront. It was a place my people could find refuge and a safe place for the children. Dutch was the problem solver he controlled all the workers; no matter how many times he wore suit and shook hands with the white folks, the streets constantly whispered in his ear and he would go running. He did what he did best and that was control the streets. He was never in one place to long he had to keep niggas in check in four states. Our youngest brother Careem just graduated high school he was in college at the University of Delaware, he was working on a rap career on the side. He had talent he just needed to know what he really wanted to do. Camisha worked in our social services department with Queen. The only person who didn't take part of the business was Bree. She was young and doing her thing, maybe one day she would come around. Raela was the spokesperson for the entire Reynolds Enterprise. I made sure my family and peoples were straight. The community knew where I came from and in their eyes I had turned my life around. In a way they were correct, I was no longer hands on in the street but I was the streets and old habits die hard.

I pulled out my key to open the door to Queens home. She still lived on the North Side of town. No matter how hard I tried to get her to relocate to the suburbs she wanted to stay in the heart of the city. She loved that fast life. So she brought a house near Brandywine Creek and we had it completely renovated. Walking in her home was like walking into mine it had luxurious finishing just in the city. I was happy as long as she was. I walked in and the house was silent. I went upstairs to my old room, which was still mine. I had a room in damn near everybody's crib, why I had no idea. I just did. I went to the closet and pulled out an outfit for the day took a shower and got dressed.

It was too early to wake up Queen but I needed to talk to her. I always went to her for advice I could make my own decisions, there was just something about having her input before I moved forward on certain things. I knocked on her door twice. Nothing. I turned to walk away and the door opened. Queen had her robe snug around her. She slipped through the door and quickly shut it. I shook my head in disgust. I should have known. Roy must have been laid up. He was probably high.

"Hey baby." She kissed my cheek, "what you doing here this early. I thought you would be home with the kids chillin." She said as she walked down the steps. Queen was too cool. I followed behind her.

"Man mom, I would but shit got real for me in the wee hours. I woke up in a great mood, I worked out, I looked up at the T.V and I saw my apartment building in a blaze."

"What!"

"Yeah, I ran out with nothing but my workout shit on went to the apartment and your mom everything is gone." I said taking a seat on the couch.

She sat down next to me with a look of disbelief on her face.

"Then I get a call from Raela,"

"Raela? You tell her imma cuss her ass out for not coming to my party. Stacey told me she was coming and the hussy ain't never show up!" she snapped interrupting me.

"Mom not right now, look the house on Apple Street got ran up in they took all of the barrels, not one is left. Marco was in their fucking some bitch and she set him up. He was found behind the BP shot in the leg."

"What the fuck was he doing behind the BP Dorian? Who was the girl? This shit don't sound right. You sure he ain't have nothing to do with it? Because if they took all of those drugs and he was fucking ole girl, they should have killed him not just shoot him in his fucking leg and leaving him there," she began to rock back in forth. If she could she would go up to the hospital and finish him off herself. That's one thing Queen couldn't tolerate -that was a snake as bitch or nigga. Loyalty was everything. "Ya'll was paying this little nigga more than he deserved as far as I'm concern. His mom lives in one of the houses on Union street right?"

"Yeah she does."

"I'm going to pay her a visit today and let her know she better talk to her son, because if she don't her ass is going to be out before she can blink. That shit don't sit right Prez, I want answers." She banged her fist on the table. "And that fire was no coincidence it was a fucking diversion!"

The situation was serious but I couldn't help but laugh. Queen was no joke. I thought about her last words. She had a point. Why didn't they just kill him and the chance of a fire and being robbed was too much. My mind went to Neka. I had to get to my phone to see if she called. She had been to the Apple street location a few times. I doubt if she was smart enough to be able to pull something like this off. I made a mental note of everything I needed to talk to Raela. If Neka did have something to do with it that bitch wouldn't live to see Christmas.

CHAPTER FOUR

A week had passed before we were able to talk to Marco. He didn't do well in surgery so he stayed a few nights in intensive care in critical condition. Raela went to pay him a visit a few hours ago. Unfortunately, he tried to play like he had amnesia when she questioned him about the night of the hit. Of course that didn't sit well with Raela. I was in my living room with a patron bottle and two double shot glasses waiting for her arrival. Neka resurfaced three days after the fire. She finally called me from her sister's house out Lexington Green, begging to see me. I asked why she didn't call me after the fire. She claimed she was so hurt by my comments that she didn't want to be alone, so she went to her sisters' house. She and her sister went back the next day to get her things and found the place was gone. I found that hard to believe since Lex was damn near around the corner. This was Delaware and news traveled fast. She went on to complain about how she lost everything. She had no clothes left and nowhere to go. Either she was crazy or slow; she should have known better than play the damsel in distress card with me. That broad made good money and had great credit. She didn't need me and I wasn't going to let her make me think that she did. I was happy that she was physically ok. After I made sure she was good I quickly ended the call. That didn't stop her from trying to contact me. She flooded my inbox with messages and texts. It was sickening. I could not stand a desperate broad.

"Front door" my security system informed me that the door had opened. The clink-clank of her designer shoes tapping the Brazilian Cherry Wood flooring echoed though out the house. I opened the bottle of Patron and filled our glasses. As I began to put the top back on she took hold of my hand.

"I think you need to keep that off. I hope your schedule is clear we are going to have a long day." She picked up her glass, and tossed the drink back in one gulp. "Pour me another." She flopped down in the chair across from me kicking off her heels. Raela looked exhausted.

I poured her drink and got up to hand it to her. I walked around the back of the chair and began to massage her neck and shoulders. Her neck was tight and I felt bad for her. Raela was thirty years old with no children and no man. She was a jewel who had not yet been discovered because of the hectic life she lived. Her life consisted of taking care of everybody and their issues. Although she looked the part of having everything, she was missing one thing, the only thing that really mattered to a woman and that was to have a family. Many times the thought would cross my mind to not have her do so much, but she was the only person I trusted. I couldn't see myself letting anyone else into our business. Even though I would never admit it, the thought of her having another man's back the way she had mine didn't sit well with me. Call me selfish. I knew one day it would come to that but until that day comes things will remain the same.

"Umm, that feels so good, but we have work to do." She broke away from my grasp and put her briefcase on the table and opened it.

"I was just trying to help you out babe," I patted the back of the recliner turned and walked back to my seat.

"I know honey it's just so much we need to go over and if you kept it up I would be in this chair knocked out." She sorted through her documents.

I sniggered, "So what's up with Marco."

Her face hardened. "Dorian, that mother fucker knows something. He tried to kick this amnesia shit with me. I had to remind his dumb ass that his thigh ain't have shit to do with his brain."

"So he's saying the shot to the leg fucked up his memory?" I tried to make sure I was hearing her right.

"Boy bye," she swatted the air with her hand and twisted her lips to the side, "he kept implying that he didn't know anything about a female being at the house. The only thing he remembers is waking up in a hospital bed. "I told him that I was going to give him another day to let the fog roll off his brain. I was on my way out the room and he sits up in his bed and says, 'No need for that Ms. Rae cause I will never remember what happened. I resign. I got a better position.' He was right cocky with it. You know me, I turned around and said, 'Excuse me, what the fuck did you just say?' You should have seen his face. The tone of my voice and my expression fucked him up. He was fumbling under his sheets for the call button. I started to go to him but before I could get close enough the nurse was in the door." Raela and I started to laugh. "He was lucky, this time" When I looked back that bastard had the audacity to wink and smirk.

"Get the fuck outta here. He set us up," I was in disbelief. I couldn't believe this little nigga fucked us with no grease. I personally got him out of the Bridge House detention center and put him in our program. That lil nigga got his GED and his charges expunged and we gave him a job. *That ungrateful mother fucker.*

"What ever happened to loyalty?"

She snorted, and then took a shot of Patron. "You know the saying, 'There is no honor amongst thieves' baby' check this out. Remember, how you asked me to look for new properties,"

"Yeah,"

"I did. You know there was three empty homes on Apple Street."

"Yeah, the one three doors down sold. I saw that." I agreed.

"Not only did that one sell, so did the other two across the street; two on Heald Street and three in Hamilton Park; they were all brought by L&G properties within the last two weeks." She tapped her pen on the table rapidly.

"Who owns L&G?"

"I checked and everything is private."

"That's not possible, that's public record." I retorted.

"You're correct, but they don't have to disclose everything on the name. For contact information it just says they are a legit company. All I have is an email address." She pulled out her laptop.

"Do some research and find out who this company belongs to. It may be nothing, but you can never be too sure." I sat back on the couch and twirled my locks. I know it may have seemed like a feminine trait; this helped me concentrate.

Marco had grown an extra set of balls; this wasn't even his demeanor which means something or someone gave him courage. He better pray that whoever he was protecting would be able to stop the reaper from paying him a visit. Death was in his near future but not until I received the information I needed. He may not talk, but as they say actions speak louder than words.

"Are you ready for the ceremony this weekend?" Raela asked, while she typed away.

Damn. I totally forgot all about the ceremony. My birthday was Saturday and I had plans to go to Atlantic City for the week to relax and do a little gambling and shopping. November, was the beginning to my busy season. It was election time,   Thanksgiving and then Christmas. My organizations held many events during this time and I had to be there to kiss babies and shake hands. I wouldn't have a break again until late January.

"My birthday is Saturday, I was going on vacation." I said, "Can't you go accept the award for me?"

Raela looked up at me and snickered.

"Well, I could but I won't. Dorian, you are being presented with a prestigious award given by the governor's office. Do you realize what that means? You will be there with a smile on your face. Celebrate your birthday later; besides, you probably weren't going nowhere but tired ass A.C." she said in a matter of fact manner.

"You are so damn smart." I threw a pillow at her playfully. She dodged it and laughed. We continued our meeting which lasted until the wee hours of the morning. She didn't leave that night; she stayed in the Ariel's room. I stood by the door and watched her sleep. I sent God a thank you. Without her I don't know if I could be able to do all of this. She was truly a blessing.

CHAPTER FIVE

"Happy Birthday, Daddy!" All four of my children sang in unison. We were gathered around the island in the kitchen as I stood in front of a huge red velvet cake shaped in a dollar sign covered in red fondant icing with metallic silver embellishments. It was hot.

"Ariel, you never cease to amaze me," I pulled her into my chest and kissed her on the forehead. She blushed.

"I can't take all of the credit. Darianna, made the icing from scratch." Darianna beamed with pride. I pulled her in for a hug as well.

"Ya'll keep up the good work and I might start you girls a cake baking business. It's big money in that you know."

They clapped their hands together and cheered. I was serious about what I said. I believed in investing in my kids' future, besides; Ariel had a gift when it came to baking, cooking period. She was to graduate this year. I figured they could start off with special orders and holidays.

Lil Dorian, lit the two candles one shaped in the number three and the other was a two. He placed both candles on the cake.

"Make a wish," my youngest son Prince said.

"I don't need a wish I have everything I need," I blew out the candles.

"Except a wife," I heard Ariel whispered.

Darianna shot her a look of death. "He doesn't need a wife he has us." She snapped.

I laughed it off, "I'm good, maybe one day but not now."

I cut the first piece of cake and put it to the side. They could take care of the rest of it. I wasn't really a sweets eater. I was getting older and taking care of my health was a serious matter. Diabetes, heart disease and other fat related illness ran heavy in my family. I didn't have time to battle illness along with the other issues that came my way. It was a little after twelve and I had a long day ahead of me. Tonight I had to be at the governor's mansion in Dover for the awards ceremony. Afterwards my brothers wanted to stop by Gary's to have a few drinks.

Raela was out picking up my suit and getting her dress for tonight's event. I still had to shoot up to Wilmington to see my mom. I tried to get Misha to bring her down to see me, but she had a million excuses of why she couldn't do it. I thought about Careem, but he was doing a show at some little rinky dink club in Philly. He was really trying to get into this music business. I talked to Gary and we were looking for a studio so he can do it the right way. It was a new business venture and we would sure to make money because now everyone in Delaware was a rapper. I ain't knock em'.

I went upstairs to get my keys and wallet so I could head to my hairdresser to tighten up my dreads, get a fresh line up for my hair and beard. I had to make sure I was right. I could never get caught slippin'. I walked in my room and grabbed my possessions on my way out my phone rang. I answered it on the first ring.

"Hello,"

"Happy Birthday, Baby" her voice dripped with seduction.

I shook my head and grunted.

"Thanks, Neka. What's up with you?"

"I want to see you tonight. I got something for you," She moaned.

"That's what's up. I got something to do tonight though, and besides I told you I can't fuck with you like that. You play too much." I said, to be honest I was about due for some pussy. I couldn't go there with her because she was clingy. I didn't want her getting the wrong idea.

"Don't act like that Prez, I just want to see you no strings attached. I really miss you. I need closure I just want to feel you inside me one more time, baby," she whined.

"How about I think about it and I'll call you after my situation tonight."

"Ok, I'll call you later." She said happily and hung up.

I placed the phone in my coat and headed out the door. I know I was making a mistake but sometimes that other head is strong willed and over powers the mind.

*****

I pulled up in front of the mansion and handed the valet my keys. Raela was standing in front of mansion waiting for me looking absolutely stunning in a Badgley Mischka color block sequined tank gown. Her hair was swept up in a loose up-do and her make-up flawless.

I walked towards her and we locked arms. I gently kissed her on the corner of her mouth.

"You look beautiful as always," I whispered.

"You're not too bad yourself. Armani always look good on you," she stated admiring my suit.

"I was starting to think you had a deal with Giorgio Armani."

I smiled and we walked in together.

The place was packed with plenty of white faces; white rich faces and a sprinkle of color. Classical music filled the air, cocktail tables drape in fine linin were scattered throughout the semi-lit reception area.

"May I offer you a drink, sir?" A young Hispanic woman asked wearing a navy blue and white maid's uniform. I took a glass of champagne.

"Thank you," she smiled and nodded.

"She didn't offer me one." Raela teased.

"Maybe she only likes Armani."

We both shared a laugh.

"I see some people I need to talk to, I'm going to leave you for a moment I will see you inside." She squeezed my hand and was off. I stood there for a moment sipping my drink and taking in the sites. There were a lot of heavy hitters in the room. I knew Raela would have all of their business cards and would have set up several meetings before the night was over. This was a good thing. I went over to the table and got another drink. While I was standing there I felt someone brush against me. I turned around and it was Monica, she worked in the secretary of the states office. She was a blonde that had a thing for me for years. She was good looking but not my type. Her husband was a politician in Kent County.

"Hello, Mr. Reynolds. Congratulations on your accomplishments." She smiled lustfully.

"Monica, thank you. How is your husband?"

She grinned.

"He's alive and around here somewhere," she moved in closer. "Mr. Reynolds it's a beautiful night tonight. A walk in the garden would be delightful, don't you think." She said in a hush tone brushing her fake triple D's against me. Her breath smelled of hard liquor and mint. I backed away from her.

"Maybe another time; excuse me for a moment there is someone I need to see." I left her standing there and went towards the crowd of men that belonged to the Wilmington Urban league. Monica, was too much. I would not have minded for her to wrap her thin lips around my mans but her husband wasn't fond of niggers and the parts where they were from white sheets were still in effect.

Forty-five minutes and six drinks later the ceremony was starting. Raela took her seat next to me at the recipients' table and waited for my award to be presented. I found myself trying to keep myself from falling asleep. If Raela didn't nudge me I would have been out a few times. When it was time to present my award the presenter announced the person who would do the presentation. I didn't pay attention until I saw her arise from the table. I swear she was the baddest dark skin broad I had ever seen in my life. She had a short haircut that was fierce, her skin was flawless it reminded me of someone of mid-eastern decent. The site of her made my dick grow an extra inch.

"Who is that?" I whispered to Raela.

"Isn't she stunning? That's Lourdes Laveau, she is new on the political scene. Tonight was the first night I met her in person. I heard about her but I never knew she was black. I also heard that she may run for senate in the next election." She informed me.

"Senate?"

"Yes, Senate" she repeated.

I was ready to say something else but she hushed me.

When she reached the podium she began to speak. She was very articulate when she spoke. She talked about me as if she knew me all my life. I was moved. The more she talked the harder my dick got.   This broad had me open with her words. She turned to me lifted the plaque and said, "This year's governor humanitarian award goes to the birthday boy, Mr. Dorian Reynolds." The way she said my name was so sexy. The fact that she knew my birthday was a surprise as well. I wonder what else she knew about me.

The room stood up and gave me a standing ovation. I went to stand up but I realized that my dick was poking through my pants. Raela looked down and noticed my issue. She stood up immediately and went and retrieved the award for me. I was so happy that we didn't need to do any acceptance speeches because I was going to look like a pervert walking up there like that. After the show we ate dinner and mingled. Before leaving I was going to make it my business to talk to Ms. Laveau.

My wish was granted as we stood in line to retrieve our coats from check out.

"I can't believe your shit got hard like that over that chick." She said with a tinge of jealousy in her voice.

"Oooh, you mad," I teased.

She punched me in the arm and rolled her eyes.

"Far from mad sweetie, more like embarrassed; you know better. If I didn't know any better I would have thought you were Dutch. That's his type shit." She scolded me.

The check-out person handed us our coats. Raela turned around and I helped her in her floor length mink. I had never seen Raela act this way and I thought it was cute. As I was putting my coat on Raela cleared her throat and nudged me. I turned around and the woman that made me rise was coming towards us.

"That's a Naeem Khan she's wearing, that dress is well over seven thousand," she whispered.

I didn't care what it was she was wearing it well; the gold gown had a beautiful rose print, the bodice was fitted accentuating every curve she possessed, it flared at mid-thigh. Although she was covered completely it left nothing to the imagination. I knew what she was working with. Her ass was a perfect heart shaped. I wanted to dive in between all of it.

"Hello, *Mrs.* Reynolds," she extended her hand out to Raela but kept her eyes on me.

"She's not my wife," I spoke up.

Raela looked as if she wanted to rip my head off.

She gave a fake laugh, "I'm not his wife we are business partners and *very* close friends." She said, with a bit of attitude. "I told you when we met earlier this evening that the recipient was my partner."

"Oh, I apologize for making the assumption of you two being a couple. There are many couples that actually do business together these days." She slowly inspected me. "You complement one another well."

As she took a sip of wine she locked eyes with me.

"That was a beautiful speech that you gave earlier. I felt like you really knew me. You blew me away when you threw my birthday in there. How did you know?"

"I do my research Mr. Reynold's there's not too much I don't know..." she smoothed her lips together and looked me over. I could see that she was feeling me as much as I was feeling her. There was an attraction, why I don't know. I knew I had to have her.

Raela stood to the side watching us gawk at each other.

"Dorian, I'm about to go. Do you need anything else from me tonight?" she put her coat on annoyed.

"No you go ahead. I think I'm going to stick around a little while longer." I said not taking my eyes off of Lourdes.

Raela turned on her heels and stormed off.

"Is she ok?" Lourdes asked.

"She's good." I assured her.

"Dorian, would you like to take a walk with me in *my* garden?"

"I would love too," I replied.

CHAPTER SIX

"Lay down next to me," Lourdes demanded. Her naked chocolate body glistened in the moonlight. Our walk in the garden led us to a small cottage not far from the mansion. Things moved so fast, I went to the bathroom and came back to see this lovely site. I removed my clothes in a haste not thinking twice.

I laid next to her on the bed; she arose to her knees and placed my throbbing ten inches in her hand. She stroked it gently before placing her plump lips around it. She lowered her head suctioning it deeper into her mouth, while her tongue danced along my shaft. She made love to the tip sending electric sensations through-out my body. Her head was so good she had me clawing at the sheets like I was some type of bitch. She slowly twirled her neck in a seductive motion as I entered back in warmth of her moist mouth.

"Damn babe, what the fuck are you doing to me?" I moaned.

She continued to please me while caressing my balls. I felt myself ready to come but I had to hold back this shit was feeling too good and I had to get up in the pussy.

I sat up some so I could watch her beautiful face as she put in work. There was an intense look to her. She moaned softly as she took me in and out of her mouth. I never saw nothing like it. I felt precum leak from my member, she lapped it up as if it were nothing. She removed her mouth from my dick and placed my balls in her mouth and hummed.

"Oh shit!" I gripped the back of her head and tried to stay as still as possible. It was about to be a done deal for me if I moved.

She moved back to my dick and took all of me down her throat.

"Suck that shit, bitch!" she was bringing out another side.

She had no gag reflex, she used her throat muscles to stimulate the head of my dick. I was done. I let loose all in her mouth. She slid my dick out her mouth and swallowed the fluid. I pulled her close and kissed her passionately. I don't know if it was the alcohol or what but I found myself falling for this broad. If the pussy was anything like her head I might have to wife her.

Lourdes sucked me until I was hard again; which took no time. She swung her leg over my pelvis. She reached behind the pillow and pulled out a magnum condom. She opened it and placed it on my dick. She then took hold of it and slowly lowered herself on top of me mounting my dick. I could feel the muscles of her walls contracting.

She started to gyrate her hips and rock back and forth at a steady pace. The harder she rocked the tighter hers walls clasped my dick. I felt like I was receiving a massage out of this world.

"Damn baby you're the shit," I whispered. I started to fuck her back and massaged her breast taking her thick hard nipples in my mouth. Lourdes lowered herself and began to bounce wildly on my dick while running her fingers through my dreads. I felt her juices building; she was about to bust.

"Fuck me Dorian," she screamed.

I flipped her over, lifted her hips and plunged into her wetness from the back. "Oh my God!" she whimpered, as I slid my dick deep down her slippery tunnel. Lourdes's pussy clung to my dick for dear life as I stroked her. It was feeling so good inside, I grunted as I increased my speed keeping my rhythm with each thrust. Lourdes began speaking the French language as she began to buck back. That shit made me go even harder. She was so fucking sexy it didn't make sense. I was fucking her so hard her legs were shaking violently and she was collapsing. I lifted her keeping my dick inside as I turned her on her back and continued to stroke.

"Zhun swee bee ehn," she shouted out as her sweet nectar ran down her thigh. I continued my rhythm and she dug her nails into my back.

"Ahh shit," I hissed. I sucked her bottom lip and bit down gently. She moaned and pulled my hair forcefully. I felt her body convulse as I dicked her down properly. I stopped moving and looked down in her soft brown eyes, smirked deviously. Lourdes looked as if she had just taken two perc thirties my dick had her on the ultimate high. I started to make love to .her again her hips started to meet my thrust. We made beautiful music together for what seemed to be an eternity. I felt pressure build up inside of me, I was about to bust. I maneuvered in her pussy hitting her g-spot like it was familiar territory.

"Dorian, I'm cumming-oh my I'm cumming," she said between moans. She arched her back off the bed and drove her hips into me hard. She started with the French talk and her face was distorted as she jerked under me. I moved even faster until I felt my body shudder, I came and I came so hard I thought the condom was going to bust. I collapsed on top of her and kissed her romantically. I lay next to her wrapping her arms around her pulling her in close to me. She snuggled up against me like she belonged there. I kissed her forehead and tried to make sense of what happened. I had one-night stands before, but nothing like this. This broad had me on some soap opera shit. I felt a connection to her and I hadn't even known her for five hours.

****

The next morning I woke up in my bed at ten the next morning. I sat up and looked around. Everything seemed normal. I went to the bathroom to drain myself. As I passed the mirror I noticed the bruises around my neck. *Oh shit it wasn't a dream.* I pissed and washed my hands. I hurried to my nightstand and checked my phone. There were thirty missed calls from Neka, two from my brother and one text message that was sent twenty minutes ago. I checked the message it was from Lourdes.

I need to talk to you about what happened last night. I will meet you at the *R Lounge* tomorrow at noon...Lourdes

I felt some type of way. I was hoping that she didn't regret what she did. I damn sure didn't. Shit, I liked that she knew what she wanted and wasn't shy about getting it. She was a boss. She had style, established, grace, intelligence and her fuck game was out of this world. Besides Raela I had never met a woman quite like her. Speaking of Raela, I picked up the phone to call her. I dialed her number and it went straight to voice mail. That fucked me up too. I never knew Raela to be the jealous type. I was going to have to see what was up with her later. For now, I was just going to enjoy my day and reflect on the best birthday sex I ever had.

CHAPTER SEVEN

The next day I woke up at my normal time and did my normal morning regimen. Last night I had dinner with Queen, she was upset with me because this was the first time that she had missed seeing me on my birthday. She made me a big dinner with all of my favorite foods. My brothers stopped over and had drinks with me. Raela showed up and she was her regular self. She talked about the awards ceremony, I thought she would bring up Lourdes but she said nothing about her to my surprise. She and Gary went off to talk about business. They gave me a pass to enjoy my day. I knew they would fill me in later.

All my kids went home except Ariel, she and her mother were going through something. I told her she could move in here. I think she was going to take me up on the offer. She was better off with me anyway. I let her drive the van to school so I didn't have to worry about her. I didn't have much to do this week because I cleared my calendar. I was supposed to be in Atlantic City on vacation. I would take this week to chill and hang out with my family. And see what the Lourdes broad was about.

At eleven thirty on the dot I pulled in front of the Rebel Restaurant. I checked myself to make sure my hair was neat and face was good. I was straight. I wore a burgundy Alexander McQueen leather sports jacket and a light burgundy Geno Slim Corduroy Pants by True Religion. I had on nice polo shirt under the jacket. I was fly as always. I walked in and I noticed her sitting in the corner by the window. She was wearing a black business suit with a pair of glasses reading the paper. Even when she was in business mode she was bad. I walked over to the table. She looked up sat the paper down and stood up. I went to hug her and she hit me with a hand shake. Talk about mixed signals.

"Hello, Mr. Reynolds how are you today?" she said politely.

I was confused like a mother fucker I didn't know how to respond. "I'm good."

She looked around before taking a seat.

The waiter came over and asked if we needed anything. I ordered a shot of Patron she asked for Pierrer water with a side of lemon.

"Mr. Rey-"

"Call me Dorian," I interrupted.

"Dorian, about Saturday; I would apologize but I'm not sorry. Everything that happened because I wanted it to. You are very appealing to me. I have read over your file and have studied you and your organization for months. I love to see a black man who's come from nothing build an empire off of hard work. You amaze me," she stated.

I couldn't help but blush. She stroked the shit out of my ego.

"You are full of surprises. After the welcome you gave I didn't expect for you to say that."

She smiled. "I have to be careful; you never know who is watching. I am under scrutiny because I am going after the senate seat. These crackers don't want that to happen but my accomplishments speak for me. I'm going to get it. I get whatever I want." She smirked.

"Is that so?" I said taking my shot.

"You should know best, I wanted you and I got you," she stated in arrogance.

"Did you really? Or was it the other way around?" I challenged her.

"Humph, I doubt it. I'm a Leo and I come from a long line of strong dominant successful women." She added.

I liked her style. She was sure of herself and I loved it.

"And I'm a Scorpio and I get what I want as well. And I can relate my mother is a strong woman as well."

"I guess that's why we mesh so well together." She took a sip of her water. "I like you, and I want to get to know you better. That is if you are not already involved."

I laughed. This broad was something else.

"Are you always this straight forward? I'm the man, can I ask you out? You making me look bad here."

This time she laughed.

"I didn't mean to bruise the ego. So, I'm going to let you control the rest of this date."

"You're going to *let* me, huh?" I raised my brow.

"Oh my goodness Dorian please stop," she giggled.

"That's what you were saying Saturday," I teased.

She rolled her eyes. "No honey, I never said stop. I wanted more." Her voice got low and sexy.

"Do you really?" I asked.

"Yes," she said licking her lips.

"Now?"

She nodded her head. I called the waiter for the check.

****

I pushed Lourdes onto her back and ripped off her lipstick red Shanghai La Perla thong. Today I was going to show her how I got down. I climbed on the bed and then spread her thick thighs and dove face first in her vanilla scented pussy.

My tongue flicked her long swollen clit causing her thighs to lock firmly to the sides of my head. She moaned deeply as my tongue massaged her sweet hot box. Her body quivered and her back arched pushing her pelvis deeper into my face. She softly called my name and pulled my hair as I delivered her pleasure. I didn't normally do the oral sex thing but she was worth me taking the plunge. My goal was to drive her insane with my skills as I made love to her with my tongue.

The sensation stirred and built her climax. I could tell she was trying to hold back but her nectar was escaping leaving sweet sticking film around my beard. When she thought she was in control I took three of my fingers and inserted them in her wetness. She shouted out in ecstasy grabbing her tits and pinching her nipples she exploded in my mouth. Her body went limp and jolted from the after shocks of the blissful quake she encountered. I continued to slowly massage her pussy with my fingers. Her pussy was tight, you would have never guessed all of ten inches had dug all up in her the other day. She had that snap back pussy.

I turned her on her back, spread her legs apart, slid my arms under both thighs and lifted her to my face. I kissed both of her plump cheeks before separating them with my thick long tongue. She started her French talk again and cried out as

I tossed her salad. I slid my tongue from crack to crevice as I ate the box and ass from the back. I had no idea what was coming out her mouth but I knew it was some good shit. I was putting it on her. I had to let her know who she was fucking with. She creamed heavy again. I laid her back down on her back and put on the finishing touches. She tried to curl up in a fetal position but I pulled her legs out and went back in. I could feel her throbbing box in my mouth. If I could I would stop and pat my damn self on the back. I put in work.

I arose from between her thighs smacking my lips with a smile on my face. She looked delusional.

"You like that shit don't you," I said with force.

"I can't take anymore," her voice was faint and her breathing was heavy and rapid.

"You ain't never have a nigga put it down like me before," I was cocky with it. She didn't have to tell me. As the song said "It's written all over your face"

Lourdes looked at me with lust and admiration in her eyes. I decided to have some fun. I placed my hands behind her knees and pulled them apart as far as they could. She must have been a gymnast because her shit was wide open. This gave me full access to her pussy and ass. I took my erect thick dick and slapped it on her wet pussy. She jumped and let out a small cry. I slapped it a few more times until she moaned out of control. I took the tip of my dick traced the lining of her pussy lips. This was driving her crazy she lifted her hips trying to force me inside of her. I pinned her down and continued to tease her until she was begging for the dick. My dick throbbed as it touched her swollen clit. I then slipped my dick inside of her wet soft pussy.

We both moaned as soon as the head entered inside of her. Her walls clamped around my tool pulling me in deep. She had hell of a pussy control. For a few moments neither of us moved because of the intense pleasure.

We made love for hours until we both fell into deep sleep.

When we woke up it was past five in the evening. I was worn out. I guess I really had a lot of sexual frustration built up inside. It wasn't that I didn't like sex. I had so much with older woman in my younger days, it really wasn't a priority to me. Lourdes was the exception; she awakened something deep within. I had to have her.

"Oh my goodness I have to head back down the road. I have a ton of meetings in the morning," she jumped up from the bed and rushed towards the bathroom. I slowly sat up on the side of the bed. I was in no rush to go. I was officially on vacation.

"So you stay in Dover?" I got up and headed to the bathroom. I opened the door and she was getting the water ready for a shower.

"I have a home in Camden-Wyoming, and one here in Wilmington. My family home I inherited is in Prince George's County." She said, and stepped in the steaming hot water, "Are you joining me?" she asked.

I pulled the curtain back and got in with her. She soaped the rag and handed it to me and I began to wash her body.

"I know there is much you would like to know about me. I'm thirty-four, no children, I have two sisters who live back home, my father was a diplomat, and ambassador for Ethiopia. My father was born here in the states but his parents were born and raised in Ethiopia, when my mother found she was pregnant they came here. His parents worked hard so that he could have the best education and it paid off."

"So, that's where the politics come in at, huh?" I asked.

"Yes and no. My mother is from Saint Lucia…"

"That's where the French talk comes from," I interrupted.

"Yes, my parents met in college and fell in love. They have two complete different back grounds and the families didn't get along. After I was born, they moved to D.C. and my father started in politics. My mother wasn't really into it but she stayed. She had two more children. After my youngest sister was born; my father fell ill. Three years later on my sixteenth birthday he passed. We were fine financially because my mother's family was wealthy in Saint Lucia and my father had done well too. I decided to follow in his footsteps as well as carry my mother's family legacy." She turned around and took the rag, "Let me wash you."

"Wow you have a lot going for you. So why are you in Delaware? Why not stay in D.C?" I inquired.

"Delaware is opportunity, you should know that. You took nothing and made an empire. You did all this without falling into the belly of the beast the streets. Not too many people can say," she gently washed my back. The corner of my lip lifted. She hadn't completely done her homework, if she did she would have known how I came up. That was a good thing. Fucking with her would be like damn near fucking with the Feds. I was willing to take that chance. As long as I kept her focused on my good side she would have no reason to look for my skeletons.

On our way out the hotel I walked her to her car. I reached over and gave her kiss, "When will I see you again?"

"I have a busy schedule for the next two days. Thursday, I have to meet with your mayor and attend a few functions in New Castle County. I will be staying at my home on the riverfront. I'll call you once I'm settled this evening and we can make arrangements then." I shut her door and she blew me a kiss and drove off. I shook my head. "That is wifey right there," I said out loud.

"What!" I heard a voice shout behind me.

I turned around and it was Neka standing there with her hands on her hips her face twisted.

"Yo, what the fuck are you doing here?" I was shocked.

"No the question is, why the fuck are you having lunch with random bitches and fucking them at the Sheraton?"

"Huh, how…"

"Yeah, nigga I saw the whole thing. I was coming out the beauty academy and noticed your car. I sat and waited for you then I see you come out with this bald head bougie bitch. So I followed you here, and I know y'all wasn't talking for five hours, Dorian. Is that who you stood me up for Saturday? I had a special night planned and you just said fuck me, huh. After all I do for you…" she ranted and raved in the middle of downtown Wilmington. Too many people knew who I was for this. I couldn't believe Neka was acting like some ratchet ass hood rat broad.

"Neka, let's go. Where's your car? We not gonna do it like this." I said in a stern voice. I took hold of her arm gently and she snatched away.   "Fuck you Dorian! You fuckin' other bitches like I ain't shit. You gon' learn that you can't play with people like that. Karma is a bitch!" she cried pointing at me.

Now I was hot, "Bitch you threatening me?" I said in a hush tone with my teeth clenched.

"I promise you that you will regret the day you threw me to the side like I was nothing," she hissed and turned away.

CHAPTER EIGHT

Things had been looking good for the last few weeks Lourdes and I had been spending a lot of time together. The businesses were going great, and Dutch had been hot on Marco's trail. It seemed that he was working for someone new. He was rolling in a 2012 Impala, tinted out and rimmed up. It was a step up from the 99' Caprice he was accustomed to riding in. He still hung around South Bridge, Dutch said he was staying at a house on Harrisburg Avenue, not far from the port. The house has happened to be owned by L&G realty. The houses on Apple Street were occupied as well but no one has yet to see who resided in them. Everything seemed to be a mystery but we knew this was a calm before the storm. The percs was still moving heavy in the street. We did manage to get a spot over on Townsend Street. It was a house that we were renovating for our Queens Foundation, but it needed to be used ASAP.

Tomorrow was our Thanksgiving Dinner for the less fortunate in my community. It was held every year at the warehouse that we used to do clothes give-a-ways and other charitable things. We would have done it at the Riverfront but you know how some people don't want to go out the hood. I usually did a walk through before the camera crews and media got there. These people knew me as Prez and knew my background. Dorian Reynolds was the Riverfront dude. The two didn't mix. My family ran this. We had close friends that had catering business and ole moms that cooked at the church to do the cooking. Young people in the community did the serving. Everyone just pitched in it was a beautiful thing. I would have loved for Lourdes to be apart of this, but she went back home for the holidays. She was a busy woman. If she wasn't kicking it with the politicians she was working on her family's business. I couldn't complain because I stayed busy myself. Regardless we still made time for each other and talked on the phone everyday.

After I made my rounds at the dinner; I went home to where my mother was preparing dinner for my family. The house was going to be full today and I was going to love it. It was a shame for such a big house to be empty half of the time. My mouth watered as I thought about the candied sweet potatoes, ham, stuffing, bar-b-que chicken, chitterings, turkey, macaroni and cheese and all the delicious desserts. I know Queen was throwing down in the kitchen. Raela was there too so I know she was going to throw some Caribbean food in the mix. With her living in Miami she had become familiar with different styles of food. Queen allowed Ariel and Darriona to handle the desserts this year. I told her I was thinking about opening a dessert business for the girls. She wanted to check out their skills. I pulled up in my driveway and noticed everyone was already here. They didn't waste no time. I walked in the house and the aroma of soul food hit me immediately.

My kids, my nieces and nephews were in the theater room. I knew because the popcorn machine that was located outside the door was running. That was good at least they wouldn't be running all through the house. I hung my coat in the closet and kicked off my shoes and threw my slippers on. I noticed that everyone had lined their shoes up as well neatly in the closet. They knew that my rules were slippers or socks in the house only. I wasn't for my floors being damaged. As I entered the kitchen Queen was over the stove as predicted. I went over to kiss her on the cheek. I noticed she was cooking alone.

"Where's Raela?" I glanced around the area thinking maybe she would come from the formal dining area.

"Oh she was here about an hour ago. Her phone rang and she rushed out; said she'd be back as soon as she handled business." She continued whipping the potatoes. I pulled my business phone from my pocket to check to see if there was a missed call or text. Nothing was there.

"Where's Gary and Dutch?" I opened the fridge and grabbed a bottle of water.

"Dutch is in the basement messing with music with Careem and Gary is in the game room watching football with Misha. All the kids are in the theatre." She looked behind me. "Where's your friend?" she turned the mixer off and grinned.

"Huh, what friend?"

"The future Senator that you've been spending all of your time with; I figured you would bring her to meet the family since she's coming before business." She poured the creamy white potatoes in a turquoise ceramic serving bowl.

"Yo, Queen you're out of pocket. Nobody comes before my business you know that." I retorted.

She walked past me taking the bowl to the serving table. "I can't tell. You've been too occupied to come to meetings at the center or check on the Marco status. I know you keep your nose out of the streets but that boy is an issue. Don't forget he knows who you really are. So does his mother who lives in one of your homes." She went over to the stove and checked the meat. "Raela has been taking care of everything with Gary and that's not fair to neither one of them; especially Gary who has a full-time job and a family to take care of." She slammed the pan containing the stuffing on the stove and turned towards me with her hand on her hip. "You getting caught up with some bitch,"

"Woo-wait a minute mom, Lourdes is no bitch. As for Raela, that's her job to handle things when I'm not there. Gary is responsible for the port jobs only. He has nothing to do with what Raela has done in the streets. To be real that's Dutch's job. Raela is a smart girl and she will figure this Marco situation out. His mom needs a place to stay she'll turn on her son before she jeopardizes her situation-believe that."

We both glared at each other before I walked away from her. We both needed to cool down for a moment. I already knew what Queen's issue was. She was over protective and no female was good enough for me. As long as they were fly by nights it was all good. Lourdes was different and when the time was right she would meet the family. Things were too early right now we had only been heavy for not even a month. I couldn't lie I was feeling her to the fullest.

Gary was chillin on the couch with a case of Heineken Beer next to him watching the game on the big screen. Misha was busy on some social network typing away.

"What's going on, Izzo?" I sat next to him and he handed me a brew.

"Shit, Queen just cussed me out." I said cracking the can open.

He kept his eyes on the screen. "You should have known that was coming you been missing in action, and I had to pick up your slack. The wifey ain't feeling that shit. She with her family now. She mad"

"Man Erica, is always buggin. I don't know why y'all are mad. I missed like two bullshit ass meetings and you acting like I'm letting the empire slip. Can't a nigga live?" I shook my head and took a gulp of the ice cold brew.

"You been living- the question is for how much longer? You slippin nigga. That Marco dude is a fucking problem," He went into his pocket and pulled out a brown small envelope. He dumped the contents in my hand. Two clear crystal-like capsules fell out.

"What the fuck is this?" I asked.

"No nigga, it's that new shit that was on TV a few months back. Somebody brought it here and Marco is slanging that shit out of the crib two doors down from the one that got knocked off. He's working for them Island niggas. Our shit is about to be shut down, nobody ain't gone want no fucking percs and E if they get that." His brows were pointed downward and his face was bunched up.

"Yo, this may not even be the same thing. That shit never even hit America after all that shit went down in Haiti. The person who was making it got killed, no one else could copy it. That drug is dead. This shit is synthetic. It ain't going to last long." I laughed and took another drink.

Gary jumped up from his seat and went towards the basement, I followed behind him. Dutch was sitting at the bar pouring shot of Henny with a disturbed look on his face.

"Tell this nigga that they selling those crystal joints again and it's the real thing!" Gary was so mad that spit flew from his mouth.

"He ain't lying. That shit is realer than a mother fucker. I just got off the phone with Raela. Marco just overdosed on his own supply. Who knew he was addicted to that shit. He didn't make it." Dutch smirked and drank down his shot.

"What the fuck you mean?" I snapped.

"Word on the street is he was lacing it with his weed. Everything ain't meant to be smoked." He added. "Raela is at the hospital with his family. It's only right being as though he graduated from the program and all.

CHAPTER NINE

Marco was a Muslim so his service was two days after Thanksgiving. We made sure everything was taken care of. Raela kept her distance from me because she knew I was aware that she had something to do with him getting the laced drugs. It was not like her to handle this type of situation of taking a life without talking things over with me first. We were at the repast held at one of the rooms at our community center when I approached her. She was giving her condolences to his younger sister.

"If you need anything at all don't hesitate to call." She hugged one of the girls who broke down in tears in her arms.

"Can I borrow you for a moment?" I asked with sincerity.

Raela excused herself and followed me out of the hall.

"What's going on, sir?" she asked nonchalantly folding her arms across her chest. She looked regal in her black pant suit.

"You tell me, when did you start making life changing decisions on your own?

She snickered. "You were too busy, and when you are busy I am instructed to make decisions. That came from your own mouth. We already knew there was a problem and I made sure it was solved."

"Raela this was not about Marco at all. You were feeling some type way about the time I'm spending with Lourdes. You're jealous-admit it."

She stepped back from me looked me up and down then busted out laughing.

"I don't see anything funny!" I snapped.

"Nigga, you're funny. I could care less about you and that chick. Don't flatter yourself sweetie, if I wanted you I could have had you and you know it. I happen to care about what goes on at Reynolds Enterprises. I helped you build this empire so if you lose, I lose as well. I refuse to allow that to happen because you sniffin some bitches pussy. For someone who always says money and family comes before a bitch, I can't tell. You don't know half the shit that's been happening in the streets. We are losing out big time. Not only here but this crystal shit epidemic spread to the South as well. It so happens that it's hitting all of our areas. So, someone has a vendetta against us. I hope you not too pussy whipped because a war is coming. I suggest you gear up?" she said sharply, turned on her heels and swayed down the hall.

"I told you shit was real," Dutch said. I turned around and he and Gary were standing behind me. I guess they heard everything because they both wore disapproving looks on their face. I shook my head and stormed out the door.

***

The next day Lourdes met me at the Cheesecake Factory in the Christiana Mall. I didn't expect her back in town until the following Thursday. She called me early that morning and set up a lunch meeting.

We sat in a booth in the corner recapping our holiday.

"So how did everything go with your family?" she asked.

I wanted to tell her it was shitty but I didn't want to add her into my drama.

"It was good. We were all together so it was what it was?" I said, vaguely.

She raised an eyebrow and took a bite of her corn tamale.

"How was yours?" I asked.

"I flew in for the day and left later that evening. Something came up and I had to come back to the states. So I didn't get to enjoy my family like I wanted. It was good to see my mother. She's finally getting over my sister's death." She took a sip of water.

"I didn't know your sister died. When did that happen?" I was puzzled. "When we met you told me you had two other sisters."

"I did and my sister who was just a year younger than me died almost two years ago. She was actually murdered. I don't talk about it-at all." She took a few more mouth full of her food like it was nothing.

I wanted to know more but she made it clear that she was not going to talk about it. I changed the subject. "So they needed you back in Dover, didn't they close for the holiday?" I asked.

She grinned. "Are you interrogating me Mr. Reynolds?"

I laughed, "Naw, nothing like that. I thought you would have called me since you were back."

"The government was closed this was my other business, the one my family owns. There was an issue and I needed to make sure things were running smoothly. My other family members used to be in charge but things changed and I was the only one capable of making sure our legacy went on. I guess I'm something like what Raela is to your enterprise." She said. "Raela, is my partner. We split everything fifty, fifty if anything ever happens to me she takes over everything." I informed her. "Wow you must really trust her or in love with her for her to have so much power. Usually, the female who inherits such wealth carries the predecessor's last name." she took a sip of wine.

I smiled. She was showing jealousy. What was it with these two? They both seemed to have it out for one another on the low.

"I trust Raela with my life and I will always love her. We have been friends since we were ten years old. She holds a special place in my heart. We have not been romantically involved and we both respect each others privacy. When the time comes and I want to marry, the woman I choose has to accept it. If she doesn't then either she gets over it or it's nothing." I stated.

"So, whoever marry you has to accept Raela."

"Exactly" I said cutting into my steak.

She nodded her head. "That's deep."

"That's called loyalty," I took a bite of my steak. We continued the rest of our meal in silence. I didn't know how she felt about it. But it was what it was. No matter how much Raela and I argued, no one not even my own mother could come between us.

CHAPTER TEN

Raela was right about a war coming; however, it wasn't the one I was quite expecting. The day of the company's holiday party; all of my employees and a few city council officials were in the main hall eating our catered lunch. My daughters prepared all of the desserts; gourmet cupcakes, pies, tarts and cookies. Darianna took it upon herself to make business cards. They called themselves *The Sweets Chicks*. They had an email sign in sheet and flyers for Valentine's Day specials. They were definitely my children.

I gave all of my employee's bonuses ranging from five hundred to one thousand dollars. They all also received gift bags from Bath and Body Works.

I gave a brief speech and recognized a few over achievers with awards. A video of prior engagements that took place over the last year was about to play on the projector screen. I took my seat next to Raela waiting for the show to begin.

A nude picture of Taneka wearing a Santa hat with my name on it, with a twelve in dildo stuck in her pussy popped up on the projector screen. There was a recording of her voice and she said;

"I'm trying to not think about you during the holidays. I can't help but to think of how we spent last Christmas Eve. My pussy is dripping as I think about how I want you to be here with me. There is an underlying conflict within because I can't stand that you would throw me to the side for another after all I have done for you. Although you used and abused my mind my body desires you. I miss taking all of your abundance into my mouth, I miss the sound of me slurping the saliva from your massive dick. I miss running my fingers through your locks and make you moan as I sucked your perfect mushroomed head, lapping the pre-cum that escaped from your love hole. I remember that night you allowed me to mount your thickness and ride it mercilessly; I pounded hard although it was painful it brought me great pleasure to have the privilege to experience the moment.

My love juices came rushing in a down pour all over your shaft. I removed myself and became your filthy bitch for the night. I sip on my juices that saturate your dick to satisfy my thirst. My oral strokes are long, slow, and hard. I see you watching in amazement as I retrieve every drop of my pussy's cum from your hard-as-steel pipe. Your dick is now in full view of your eyes because I have released it and am now sucking your nuts like a baby to his mother's breast. I take your entire sack into my mouth and caress them with my tongue. I take you back in my mouth so you bust like you always do. I take my daily dose of protein like a good girl and lay back waiting for you to treat me like the ho that I am. That's what you used to call me when you fucked me your "med ho" That's all I was to you and I didn't care. Dorian, I'll be whatever you want me to be as long as I'm with you. Merry Christmas, Prez"

The sound went off. The picture was still frozen on the screen everyone was stuck in their seats. I loosened my tie. If I had a gun on me I would shoot the shit out of that screen. I had no idea how she was able to get that in here. Someone had to be working with her. When I find out who they could cancel Christmas because they wouldn't be here to see it.

Raela's eyes looked like they were about to pop from her head. I shook my head not knowing what to say. I couldn't even look at her or anyone else for that matter. People began to speak in hush tones amongst one another. Shit was about to be messy.

Raela jumped up and ran to the podium. Someone in the back cut the projector off. I made my escape while Raela did what she does best clean up my mess.

***

Two hours later I was sitting in Queen's living room getting chewed out by everyone who had a mouth to speak.

Raela paced the floor in silence. It had been a good twenty minutes and she hadn't found the words to say to me. I already knew she was thinking of some good shit to say.

"Who is she and somebody please tell me how this happened?" Raela asked sharply.

"You already know who she is." I don't know why she tried to act like she didn't know.

"Actually, I don't know. If I did I wouldn't ask you. It's not like you could see her face." She snapped.

"Yo, first of all you need to tone your voice down. I don't know who the fuck you think you're talking too." I said raising my voice. She walked over to me and stood in front of me and pointed in my face.

"I'm talking to you, Dorian and like-I-said- I don't know who it was because all I can see was her nasty ass pussy with a fake dick hanging out. That's classy-not. You sure know how to pick em!" she retorted.

Queen stood up and took Raela by the arm leading her to the other side of the room. Raela was hot tempered when she wanted to be and she knew if she didn't intervene things were going to get out of hand.

"Well who is she," Gary asked. He sat in the chair quietly observing the situation. Dutch and Misha was over in the corner cracking jokes as usual. Man, that's TaNeka..." I said dropping my head.

"I told you that bitch was going to be a fucking problem. I told you to keep it business with that bitch. Now she on some fatal attraction shit." Gary threw his hands up shaking his head.

"Oh my God, TaNeka as in A.I Dupont TaNeka?" Raela sat up in the seat like she wanted to jump on me.

Queen looked from me to Raela to Misha, "Misha, ain't that the temps name you hired to fill the nurse position at the center." She asked.

Misha looked to the sky like she was trying to find an answer, "Umm, is her last name Brown?"

"Fuck!" I shouted. "Misha, who the fuck told you to hire anyone without my permission!"

We needed a nurse because Cherron went on maternity leave. Raela told me to call the temp agency so I did. It ain't my fault that you can't control the bitches you fuck." She playfully punched Dutch in the leg and laughed.

"It's funny, huh, well guess what your ass is fired! Laugh now!" I turned around towards her and laughed sarcastically in her face.

The whole house went into an up roar.

"Fuck you Dorian, you can't fire me! My last name is Reynold's too nigga! I have rights just like you!" she shouted.

"That's where you're wrong. I own all this shit! Camisha Reynolds ain't on a mother fucking thing but a pay check-a pay check I sign." I reminded her.

"I don't need your fucking job, bitch!" Misha jumped up and started talking her shit waving her hands in the air like she was about to do something. I struck a nerve.

"Dorian, you are wrong and you need to apologize to your sister. She didn't know you were messing with that crazy ass girl. She a nurse and doing shit like that?" Queen said in disbelief.

"She probably the one who set fire to the apartment too," Gary added.

"What!" Everyone said in unison.

"Man why you have to go there?" I turned to Gary.

"I told you that Bitch was a problem. You don't listen, you think you got everything under control and you almost let a bitch ruin you. She called you, Prez on that tape Izzo. If anyone puts two and two together we over." He stated.

"There's one thing you seem to forget Dorian, this is not just your shit. I own half of everything," Raela jumped over the conversation that was going on. She turned to Misha. "He can't fire you without me agreeing so that bullshit he talking don't even matter. He's upset right now because one of his fuck buddies just made a fool out of our company. I want this girls information, she is not to step foot back on any of our properties." She turned to me. "I think my time here is up. I'm going back home and I will handle things from Miami."

"You don't need to leave," Gary said quickly.

Raela turned to him teary eyed. "I need to fix things down South, your brother has it all under control up this way. He knows how to get in touch with me to clean up his next mess." She rolled her eyes at me and walked over to Queen and kissed her on the cheek then walked out the door.

Everyone looked at me waiting for me to go out and get her. It wasn't happening Raela was grown and if she wanted to be stubborn and childish that was on her. When I didn't move, Gary grabbed his coat and stormed out the door.

CHAPTER ELEVEN

It was the end of February, Lourdes and I were officially together. I took her and Queen to the American Grill in West Chester on New Years Day so they could meet. Queen didn't say more than three words to her that evening. Lourdes tried her best to make small talk with her. Queen didn't budge, as long as she was respectful I was good.

Lourdes stayed at her condo in Wilmington most of January. I stayed with her a few nights out of the week. The time that I spent with her I learned that not only was her physical sex the shit, she was able to make love to my mind. Lourdes was a smart woman; I could really see myself settling down with her. The final test would be to see how she interacted with my kids. If she could break Darianna down to accept her, I would be on my way to Tiffany&Co. immediately.

I gave her a tour of the Recreation Center and the look on her face as we walked through showed that she was impressed. She told me she had heard about it but never expected it to be so grand. I told her I believed in doing it big or leave it alone. Although she knew all that I had done she said it was different to actually see everything in the works. Everyone stared as we walked through the hallways giggling and holding hands. My employees had never seen this side of me so I knew there was going to be gossip about who this woman was. I hoped they didn't think she was the same broad they seen spread eagle at the Christmas party.

Gary and Dutch met her briefly when they dropped me off to the airport a few weeks ago. She and I went to Las Vegas for Valentines Day. They were short on words. They wasn't fucking with me to heavy on the broad tip ever since the TaNeka situation. The fact that Raela hadn't been back since the argument didn't set well with anyone.

I hadn't spoken to her verbally since then. We only conversed through email or Gary. I didn't understand how he became the middle man all of a sudden but I wasn't going to worry about it. I was too occupied with Lourdes and the business that was going on up here. I knew Raela was stubborn and eventually she would get over it and make her way back up this way. For what I was hearing she and Dutch were busy because that Crystal drug was knocking our pill business out the way for a minute in Miami. They were able to get things in order before things got to out of control and a war broke out. Unfortunately I couldn't say the same for up here. I was on my way to meet Gary now to discuss the business or lack of I should say.

I pulled up in front of the townhouse in Becks Woods. His wife's car was parked in the driveway. I shook my head and put the car in park. He knew I hated talking around Erica. She was the type that grew up in the projects, got knocked up at fourteen and then went to college. My brother and mom took care of my niece while she was away. When she came back she was on some other shit. All of a sudden she needed to be married and didn't want her child to be raised in the hood; which was all good because mines wasn't roaming the city either but she wanted to make her forget she was black all together. She never came to any family gatherings. She hung with her white friends from the bank. She tried to get Gary to denounce his culture too. But he wasn't having it. We thought she would leave him but truth was she was a money hungry broad. Gary was the bread winner and paid for everything. She blew the money she made trying to keep up with her crew.

I hated being around her because she was fake as shit behind closed doors she couldn't stand us but when it was time to be in the spotlight she loved to say she was Dorian Reynolds sister-in-law.

I walked in the house and she was curled up on the cream leather sectional with a pink bonnet on her head reading one of those white romance novels. When she heard the door shut she moved the book down far enough for me to see her four-eyes appear over the book. She didn't have in her blue contacts. I guess she wasn't having her pink people over today.

"I didn't hear you knock," she shifted her body around on the couch.

"That's because I didn't, what's up Erica?" I greeted her.

"Well Dorian in case you didn't realize it. This is not your house, we pay for this and I would appreciate it if you knocked next time." She was being snippy.

"I hear that," I said continuing to the back not paying attention to a damn word she was saying. I left her talking to her damn self. All she wanted was attention. I wasn't in the mood to entertain her. Gary was sitting in the den watching Shottas on the flat screen with the sound turned all the way low. I shut the door behind me when I walked in.

"Why ain't you tell me she was going to be here? You could have came to my house or met at a restaurant or something. You know I don't trust her around when we discussing business,"

"Erica should be the last thing on your mind. Shit is fucked up. Our shit is not moving. That

Crystal shit is all over Wilmington. We been sitting on the same product since the end of December. We can't give the shit away," he said. The fucked up thing is they paying double what we charge for that shit. They go crazy over it."

I was confused to why I was just hearing about it if things were that bad. It was going on three months and no one had said a word.

"How did that happen? I thought I paid niggas to regulate this type shit. If you seen it was getting this bad why wasn't it stopped. What the fuck was Dutch doing all this time?" I snapped.

"Dutch was in Miami handling shit with Raela. In case you forgot I work a real fucking job and I did what I could. I tried to let you know but you was missing in action, I told Raela and because she was busy she pointed me back to you. I figured if you ain't care I wasn't going to worry about it until things got too bad and now shit is really bad. I had to stop our shipment from coming in because we don't need it,"

I couldn't believe what I was hearing. We had never been in this position. We could never keep enough product in. Hearing that we were sitting on some old shit for months was killing me.

"Does Raela know how bad it is up here?" I asked.

He nodded, "She said you can figure it out. She is handling the South right now."

I sighed heavy and sat back. I hoped she was really handling business. I would hope that she wouldn't be that petty to put business to the side.

"There is no way that they are flying it in. They have to be using the port to bring everything here. I need you to check things out,"

"Izzo, what you think I'm stupid? I been checked on that; nothing comes off those boats without me checking. It's not coming in on ships." He said. "It has to be coming through parcel."

"Well, we need to intercept it. If they want to stop our shit from moving then we are going to take their shit. In the mean time we need to think about changing up our product. I'm about to do a little research and find out who the connect is for that crystal shit."

"You ain't been around for a minute they don't only have spots by the port they all over Wilmington. I don't know where these niggas came from but they are here strong and they recruiting. If we go up against them it's going to be a war. You can't play the upstanding businessman and notorious drug lord in a city as small as Wilmington is. It's going to collide and everything will fall apart. You need to figure out what position you want to play," Gary stated.

"What you talking about nigga, I'm not new to this I'm true to this,"

He laughed, "I hear you but I can't tell. You running around here with your face all over build boards and fucking with the Politian broad. I heard she on her way to be a senator. Where do you fit in all that? You getting all serious with her, what you think she going to say about when she find out about your dark side? She's going to find out *if* you're really trying to go to war. Everybody will find out because whoever these people are, they ain't the bullshit niggas we had run ins with before. They are the real deal. They were able to snatch Marco up from us and take our shit without a problem. Raela getting rid of him meant nothing; they just added new niggas to their roster,"

"So what are you trying to say? You want out or something? You eat from the pills too," I reminded him.

"I know what my position is and I will always be good. You just need to find what lane you trying to go in and stay in it." He turned the sound up on the television and finished watching his movie. I understood what he was saying. Truth be told I didn't need this money but this was where I was from and no out of Towner's was going to come and set up shop in my shit and stop my money. I was Queen's child, royalty and we didn't bow down to anyone in the past and I wasn't going to start now.

CHAPTER TWELVE

"So, was the track hot or what?" Careem asked beaming. We were in the new studio I built out in Pike Creek. It was premier, it had state of the art equipment. Gary had put together a record label called Cash Talk Entertainment. I was a silent partner in the movement. I already had my hands tied in too much.

To be honest I think this is why Gary really didn't care about what was happening in the streets. He was trying to go hard with Careem with his music. It would definitely be a good look because the boy was hot! He was still in school at the University but he had booked a show down in Daytona Beach for Spring break. Gary was his manager and was going with him. He was leaving in two days and wanted me to hear his tracks before he left.

"Yeah you got it. The question is are you ready?" I asked trying to see where his mental was at.

"Damn right I'm ready! Music is my passion and I can't see myself doing nothing else besides it. I already talked to Queen about school. She gave me her blessing as long as I agreed to stay in school until I get major distribution. Man, I have never been so focused," he assured me.

His words were sincere and his expression said it all. This is what he really wanted to do. He was ambitious so I knew he would go far. Careem was a good kid. He didn't do drugs wasn't in the streets but he was a product of the streets. What he rapped about was real; no one could ever say he was one of those fake me outs. If need be he could be about that life as they say; it was in his blood.

It had been two weeks since I spoke to Gary about the problem we were having. After our meeting I called Dutch and briefed him on the situation. He didn't sound surprised about anything. Unlike Gary he was a wild card and down for making an example out of a nigga. He was in North Carolina, he let me know that business was moving smoothly there and he would move the left over product down there.

The Crystal hadn't made an impact like it did here in Miami yet. He let me know that he was meeting Gary in Daytona for Careem's show and he would fly back with them. He sent a few of his best soldiers from down South up to meet him so they could handle the situation when he returned.

Careem went back in the booth to do another track. Gary tapped me on the shoulder and nodded his head towards the exit. I grabbed my bottle of water and slipped on my black leather jacket and followed him. The door opened and it felt like my lungs had frozen.

"Damn it was just sixty degrees earlier!" I complained. Gary unlocked the doors to his Platinum Range Rover. I entered on the passenger's side.

"Man, turn this heat on. It's cold as a bitch," I said blowing into my hands rubbing them together.

Gary chuckled, "Ain't nobody tell you to come out with that little ass jacket on, looking like Meek Mill." He turned the car on and put the heat on blast.

"*Ha*-funny you got that," I laughed along with him. "So what's up?"

"Erica just called me beefin' Dutch recruits pulled up to the crib like twenty minutes ago," soon as he said that his phone rang. He looked at it and turned it so I could see Erica's face. He pushed end and threw the phone in the console.

I rested my hand in my dreads, as I tried to figure out what the fuck was on Dutch's mind. He knew damn well out of all places Gary's should've been the last place on the list.

"What the fuck is on your brothers' mind?" Gary asked with a disgusted look on his face.

"Man, I don't even know but ain't no use in trying to figure it out what's done is done. Call them niggas and give them the address to my crib over Northside. They can stay there and lay low until Dutch comes back up with yall." I said.

"Why don't they stay at the motel? Staying at the crib is not a good look," he rebutted. "What if someone catches on to them and follow them back to the crib. Don't forget that is where Raela stays when she is here. We don't need anyone retaliating and she end up getting hurt." His eyes became leaden as he glared in the review mirror. His demeanor threw me to the left. I noticed that whenever we talked about Raela he would get the same look. I made a mental note to check him on it later.

"Where should they stay then? I don't think it should be none of the motes on the Ave. too much shit be going over there. They need to be on the low."

Gary nodded. "Have them check in the American Inn on route forty. That's right next to the highway. It's in the cut not to many people fool with it so they should be good."

"You right. Google the address and tell them niggas to get a room there and I will meet up with them in a few."

Gary picked up his phone and got right on it.

CHAPTER THIRTEEN

I ended up meeting King and Blaze at the American Inn the next morning.

When Gary called to tell them the change of plans they expressed they were tired from being on the road; after there beef session with Erica they couldn't take on much more that night. I laughed when they told how she went off on them. She went as far as threatening to call the cops if they didn't get off her property. I wasn't surprised that was typical Erica. It didn't help that one of her friend's from the job was over with her kids. I know they was probably scared to death when they saw two big bama ass niggas with thick dreads and mouth full of platinum and golds. I wish I was there to see it all go down. Gary said she bugged out so bad when he got home, he had to go stay at Queens to prevent himself for going upside her head.

I knew she must have really performed because my brother wasn't the type to lay hands on a broad that was Dutch's steelo. He'll slap a broad in minute without thinking twice; like I said that nigga was a wild card.

I picked up King and Blaze in my squatter; a tinted out navy blue Mercury Sable. It was nothing flashy about it which meant it would blend in well while we checked things out. We drove over to Apple Street and parked the car at the end of the street to watch what was going.

"Bruh, is this where those boys be at?" King nodded his head towards the house on the corner while rolling his blunt.

"That's one of them." I tapped on my side window, "This house right here on the end and the one next to it. That's their spot too. I'm not sure which one if not all has the biggest stash."

"Dutch said these boys done took over the city, this here don't look like the whole city." Blaze said from the back.

I chuckled, "Naw they have at least two to three spots on each side of town and a few spots out New Castle." I informed them. King lit the blunt and took two tokes before passing it to Blaze.

He bent over holding his chest coughed. It sounded like he was about to throw up his lungs.

"Yo, you alright."

He coughed again then blew out smoke. "Bruh, I'm good that shit is kill."

I didn't smoke weed or do any type of drugs. I stuck to the alcohol and I didn't fuck with that all the time. I had to keep my head clear. I used to dabble in weed game back in the day and sometimes if I came upon a deal, I let my lil cousins get some pocket change by throwing them a few pounds of the exotic. It didn't bring in enough money for me. The pills I would triple my money and people love this shit.

"They're making that dough over here; I done counted like thirty people coming in and out of these two cribs in the last fifteen minutes. Then it get's quiet for about half an hour before another thirty or so come." Blaze was leaned back against the door watching the traffic."

"Yeah they are killing them. What's fucking me up is I'm seeing way too many familiar faces. I've watched three of my tenants roll up in there." My right temple started to pulsate as I thought of all the money I was losing. I couldn't watch no more of this shit I started the car up.

"Where we fittin' to go?" Blaze sat up. "I ain't done checking shit out. We still don't know who we need to get yet, Bruh"

"I have to show you all the areas. We still have to check North, East and West Side. Tomorrow we can go to New Castle."

I drove over to Second and Rodney and parked on the corner. It was two houses right next to each other and bitches and niggas sat on the porches in the cold waiting to get in. Like clock work it went the same way except it was double the amount of people. They would go in three at a time. They stayed in the house no longer than two minutes. The same went for every other part of town. You never saw the dealers only the customers. There was no one on the streets selling this shit. They had some type of system set up. We were out until about nine o'clock that night. I took them back to the hotel. Gary called to see what we had come up with. I told him what we discovered and he got quiet on me. A few minutes later he said. "Izzo we can leave this shit alone. Careem is ready to come up in the industry and we got more than enough money.

We getting to old for this shit. Let Dutch do this shit from the South we still got that territory. You got a good thing going with the senator broad just sit back and chill. We good, Izzo."

I moved the phone away from my ear and stared at it. I know I wasn't talking to big G's son. I know his dad had to be turning in his grave. He was on some old Bitch shit. Hearing him talk like that made me more determined to shut these niggas down.

"Gary man, like I told you before if you want out. I give you my blessing. I can't let some mother fuckers think it's ok to shut my shit down. We lookin' like straight suckers right now. I'm going to handle this shit. Watch what I tell you. I'm going to send these niggas back to picking bananas." I started to laugh.

"You know what it's late. I'll hit you tomorrow after I come home from *work*." He hung up the phone.

I threw the phone on the passenger's seat. I grunted that nigga ain't have shit to say because he knew I was right. I wasn't doing this just for me it was for the family. We had a legacy to protect. If I let this go every nigga round here would get tough; next thing you know they would be running up in my peoples cribs. I know the streets was talking and I wasn't even in them like that. That was all going to change; even if I had to go back in the streets to fix it myself.

CHAPTER FOURTEEN

Two weeks went past. Blaze, King and I had collected information but had not made a move. It was like we were playing a chess game we had to strategically map things out before making a maneuver.

I rented four cars so we could switch up so people wouldn't get suspicious. We decided it was best for us to split up. Blaze took South Bridge, and New Castle, I took West side since it was close to the center. King did the East and North Side. We stayed on them heavy taking notes, watching who was who; for a minute it felt like I had my own private investigation team.

My time with Lourdes was limited and when we were together physically my mind was on the money that was being stolen from me by the minute. One particular night we were in the midst of getting it in; Lourdes was on top trying her hardest to please me.

My shit just wasn't working every time she got it hard after two or three strokes my dick was dead. After several attempts she rolled off and turned her back towards me. I just laid their staring at the center trying to wrap my mind around my dilemma in the streets. Ten minutes later she jolted up and snatched the sheet from her body. Her feet slapped loudly against the hardwood floors breaking my attention. I turned toward her in time to watch her slide into her panties. She grabbed her jeans that were draped over a chair in her sitting area.

"What's up? Where you going?" I sat up in the bed.

"I'm going on the balcony I need some fresh air." She had her jeans on threw on a shirt and put on her UGG boots in a haste.

I scratched my head and looked out the window. It was pouring down raining. I picked my watch up from her night stand the time read two in the morning. What the fuck?

I climbed out of bed and put on my boxers.

"Babe, what's up with you? It's pouring down raining and it's late. You gon' catch a cold."

Lourdes gave me a weak smile, "I'm fine Dorian. Are you ok?"

"I'm good babe."

"Really?"

"Yeah, why you say that," We were now standing face to face I leaned in to kiss her and she backed up. "Babe, what's wrong why you backing away from me?"

She bit her bottom lip took a deep breath, looked to the sky and shook her head.

"Dorian, is there something that you're not telling me?"

I didn't know what to say. Did she find out about the real me? I stood there silent trying to figure out what she was really asking me. Her eyes started to glisten and my heart sank. I reached for her.

"No babe, you know everything you need to know about me. What made you ask that?" I held her in my arms, I felt her body shudder in my arms. "Babe, I love you." She pulled away and looked me in the eyes.

"What did you say?" Tears and snot was on her face. I took my hand a wiped it away.

I looked her in the eyes, "I said- I love you." The truth was I knew I had fallen in love with her months ago. I just didn't know when the right time was or how to tell her. I was actually scared. The only other women I ever loved outside of family was Amber and Raela. The love I felt for Lourdes was different. I couldn't explain it. I knew she felt the same way about me. She didn't have to tell me. The actions during the time we spent together spoke volumes.

"I love you too, Dorian. I wanted to tell you this for a minute. I got scared these last few days because you seem different. It's like your mind is somewhere else. I was afraid it was someone else."

I hugged her tight. "No I'm good. I have a lot going on with my company right now. There are so many decisions I need to make and with Raela working in the other office everything is on me."

"I understand completely. My life is complicated as well that's why I never got serious with anyone. I never intended to fall in love with you. I was looking for a boy toy to take of the edge," she admitted.

I stepped back, "Damn, Lourdes you was going use me for dick. Now that's fucked up." I shook my head and started to walk away.

She ran after me laughing, "Stop Dorian," she gripped my arm. I pulled away playfully. I acted like my feelings were hurt. I sat on the side of her bed with my arms folded.

"*All you want from me is a one night stand,*" I sang Father MC's old song.

She picked up a pillow and hit me with it. She fell into my arms and we made love just like they do in the movies.

The next day she headed off to D.C for a week long conference. That was good for me. We had both admitted that we loved each other and wanted to be together. We agreed to continue to keep things going the way it was. We both were busy and needed to get our other lives in order before making any major decisions. This would give me time to try and figure out how I would get her to accept the other side of Dorian Reynolds-Prez.

CHAPTER FIFTEEN

"You mean to tell me that these niggas got fucking e.b.t card systems," Dutch was animated. He was talking with his hands extra hype with a blunt hanging out of his mouth. "So you mean to tell me mu-fuckas got appointment times to come swipe their mother fuckin cards to get drugs. Who the fuck are they working for the government? When did the game get so sophisticated?" King fell out in laughter. They both got a kick out of what was going on. Blaze, Gary and I sat around stoned faced watching the Black Beevus and Butthead.

Wasn't shit funny. I was beyond pissed. I couldn't believe my eyes when Blaze brought me the card the other day. He had got it from some stripper broad that worked at Hak's. He saw her go to the house everyday to pick up her drugs. One day he decided to follow her and her trail lead straight to the dusty strip club.

He showered her with ones two nights in a row on the third night. She told him she could give him a private show at the raggedy motel across the street from the strip joint. He took that as a way to get in. He waited until she got off of work instead of taking her to the motel. He took her to the Courtyard in Downtown Wilmington. He said when she noticed they was headed in that direction she asked him to stop by one of the houses so she could get something. He said she pulled out a gold card that resembled a credit card. She knocked on the door went in and came back out.

When they went to the Hotel he said they blew a few L's and he watched her slip the crystal rock like pill under her tongue. She offered him some he told us he said he was cool.

He said five minutes later she was a whole other person she was talkative, extra horny, and yet relaxed.

He said he ain't ever seen no shit like that before. She answered all of his questions. We knew that there was no money spent at the houses everything was done through the card. He told us she said she could load her car at any check cashing place that took money gram. When she went inside she swiped her card and pin number and she picked how much she wanted to spend up to five hundred dollars. Once she made her purchase the drugs were dispensed from the "vending" machine.

She told him they weren't American but they were black. She said they spoke with a West Indian accent and there were three to five of them in there at a time.

I couldn't believe the shit I was hearing. These were no ordinary drug dealers.

Blaze said he stayed and watched her to see how long the high lasted. He said it was good for about three hours before she needed another hit.

"So if they have all of that going on. What did they need Marco for?" Gary asked.

"Shorty said, they use the local dough boys as salesmen. They give them testers to hand out to people they know get high. They pay them good. Cuz, I'm telling you I don't see no doughboys on the corners at all." Blaze chimed in.

Gary looked at me and shook his head.

"How are we going to stop that, Izzo?" he grunted. "What we run up in the spot spraying niggas and walk out with a fucking Vending machine on our back? This is bullshit. I ain't never in my life heard no shit like this before. If anybody told me some shit like this existed, I would have sworn they was fucking lying. I'm telling you now ain't a fucking thing we can do. Leave this shit alone."

Everything that Blaze said was processing in my head. Gary's words had fallen upon death ears. I needed to know who the fuck was the mastermind behind their organization. Whoever it was loaded. There was no way no regular niggaz was pulling this off. My money and resources wasn't even on that level. I knew in order for them to keep an operation like this up they had to be making big money. I guaranteed they was making millions monthly.

I shook my head. *Naw Prez, you can't let these niggas get away with this.* If I couldn't take their shit now; I was going to stop them until I figured out how I could.

I turned to Dutch, "I need you to send for ten of your best soldiers from the South. I need them here by Friday."

"That's not a problem." He was leaned back in the chair calmer. "What you got in mind lil brother."

I turned to Blaze, "Tell me how you got your nickname again?"

Blaze rubbed his hands together with a sinister grin on his face. "I see we think the same way, Bruh"

I smiled and gave him dap.

"You niggas is crazy. If you need me I'll be in the studio." Gary put on his coat and walked out the door. Everyone turned to me. I threw my hands in the air. "We have to choose our own battles wisely. He chose."

Everyone nodded in agreement.

Dutch clapped his hands together. "Alight game time!"

CHAPTER SIXTEEN

Operation Blaze and Glory...

I sat at the head of the of a mahogany board room table located in the basement of my secret location; staring at thirteen ravenous faces. Their desire for anarchy was about to be appeased. The past week we shut ourselves away from the world to cautiously strategize the demise of our opponent.

Blaze was chosen to lead the brigade due to his knowledge and skill of operating explosives; courtesy of the good U. S. of A's army.

We had everything from C4 to hand grenades to set it off. We had gunners on deck in case anyone managed to escape the inferno. There were fifteen houses in total that were to be hit.

Most people would look at that as a handicap; our advantage was that most of the houses were side by side or across from one another. All of the men including myself had received a crash course in detonating a bomb. We needed to be at least a hundred feet in range and a click of a button would blow them and anyone to close away. My concern was children, I didn't want any kids or innocent woman to die. With that in mind, we decided to do it at eleven in the morning on a Tuesday. The children were or at least they should be in school during that time.

It was now nine o'clock in the morning and it was raining lightly. We all sat around silent in deep thought. I had no idea what was on their mind; but mine was on the aftermath. My old customers were going to come running back. I was going to welcome them with open arms but there would be a price to pay for their disloyalty. I was going to triple the price on the pills for at least a month. They made me lose money for three months. It was only right.

At nine thirty we were all going to roll out to our locations. I gave everyone a burn out cell phone and put every number in a text message group. Once they received the text with the code, 'it's a go' we would all deploy at the same time; those areas that needs extra explosives would get the grenades. Fifteen houses going up in smoke would cause mass hysteria. The Wilmington Police or Fire Department was not ready to handle anything like it. This would give us time to meet back at the hideout and collect all the phones and evidence. I never trusted anyone; not even family to clean up a job. People can be careless and in my line of work there was no room for error.

****

10:55 A.M

Blaze and I sat in the sable watching our target; the rain had picked up some but that didn't stop the feinds from copping drugs.

"It's about that time bruh," Blaze had the remote in his hand with his thumb hovering over the button. There was a demonic grin on his face. This shit was right up his alley. He had been gun ho during the entire preparation. I was starting to think that Iraq shit fucked him up a little bit. His ass needed to be in the army somewhere blowing shit up but his love for a bitch they called *Kush* lead his ass to a dishonorable discharge. He thought his life was fucked, despite his college degree, and all that other senseless shit no one was opening the doors for someone the army threw away. There was one door that remained open-the streets. The streets held no prejudice –all were welcome-there was only one rule-and that was to *Survive*.

"Yeah, I guess it is." I pulled out the burn out cell. I took one last look around to see if there was any children in sight. The block was clear except for a few junkie dudes walking towards the houses. They looked like shit. I shook my head. *I would be doing these niggas a favor.* They looked like the walking dead anyway. I sent the text. I waited a few more minutes for a response. Nothing came through. I started the car and drove off slowly. When we hit Broom Street Blaze hit the button. I was seconds away from the Safari Bar, I heard a thunderous *boom* followed by a few more loud explosions that shook the foundation.

I looked at Blaze and a huge smile was on his face. I looked in my rear view mirror a thick black cloud of smoke was making its way down the hill. The smoke was so heavy that it covered the flames. People were coming out of their houses to watch the spectacle taking pictures and recording the footage. Cars began to slow down to see what was going on. I dodged in and out of the traffic hitting the horn attempting to flee the scene.

Sirens could be heard from every direction. My cell phone began to ring off the hook. I picked it up, "Hello," I tried to sound as calm as possible. I had to admit a nigga was shook up. I did a lot of things but I had never seen no shit like this. I looked in front of me and you could see the smoke come from eastside and south bridge. It was like the smoke clouds were coming together darkening the skyline of Wilmington.

"Dorian, are you ok!" It was Queen shouting in the phone.

"Mom, I'm good. I'm the highway on my way to the center." I lied.

"No baby, turn back around. Go home! I think we are under attack or something. Its explosions everywhere.

I swear it looks like September eleventh out here. Your Aunt Tilly called me and said she was in Save A Lot and the whole Rodney Street just blew up out of nowhere. I'm hearing it did the same thing on 30th street by Rashes, wait hold on." I could hear everyone in the office panicking. She was yelling at someone in the background.

I put the phone on mute.

"Check in to make sure everyone is on 95 South-they about to shut the whole city down." I ordered Blaze.

He sent out the text. I heard Queen screaming *Hello* on the phone. I unmuted her, "Yeah I'm here."

"They said Pine Street and the whole South Bridge and New Castle was hit!" I heard her sigh deeply like she was trying to calm herself down.

"Dorian, *where* are you at again." There was a hint of unsureness in her voice.

"Look Queen, I'm good. Tell Bree and Misha to stay out of the streets. If it's ground zero like you saying shit is going to get real-fast. I'll hit you when I get to my destination. I hung up the phone.

"Everybody got out." Blaze informed me. That was a relief. Careem was at the college in Newark so he was out of harms way.

It then hit me that Lourdes was supposed to be back in town today. She called me a few days ago from D.C to let me know she would be back

Monday evening. We were supposed to meet up at her Condo. I became frustrated all over again. I dialed her number on the cell. It went straight to voice mail. I slammed my fist into the steering wheel. "Fuck!"

Blaze whipped his head in my direction, "You good, Bruh?"

I nodded my head, "I'm straight." I didn't want to get all in to my business with him.

"Yo, look how fast them state boys flying up the highway." He pointed toward the northbound lane at the twenty or so State police cars heading in the direction of Wilmington. "They got the choppers out and er'thing. They ain't gon be able to fly threw that smoke." He looked out the window and laughed.

CHAPTER SEVENTEEN

TERRORIST ATTACK OR DRUG WAR...

I read the headline in the News Journal. Two days had passed since the operation. Anything and any one who could potentially link us to the attack was disposed of; unfortunately that meant a few soldiers didn't make it home. Not everyone was built for war like we thought. The three that didn't survive were all traveling together unfortunately outside of Virginia they were in a tragic car accident.

The rest were paid and sent on their way including King and Blaze.

Dutch decided to stay in Middletown with me for the rest of the week. Wilmington was now controlled by the FEDS. Nothing was moving unless they knew about it. I closed the center down for the rest of the week. My plan was successful to a certain point; there were innocent casualties. When we blew up the houses on Rodney it reached all the way down to fifth and Rodney. We didn't think about the houses being connected to a gasolines. Every house that was connected blew.

Most of the houses were empty but a few elderly did perish. I was fucked up about it. The plan seemed to be great at first but we didn't think it all the way through. Yes, we did get rid of the competition but we brought in a new enemy-the FEDS. It would probably be months before we could set shop up again.

Gary had come by yesterday with his I told you so's that I wasn't trying to hear. He was hot because the Docks had been under federal watch since the incident.

It was reported that the exposions started in South Wilmington outside of the Port first; a two minutes later explosions came from everywhere else. One of the boys had moved too fast. So they think it has something to do with the Docks. There was a city wide curfew put in place.

The shelters were over filled with those who lost their homes. Raela found out what happened and put in a call to the Red Cross. She donated our gym to act as a temporary shelter for those who were effected. I tried to reach out to her but she refused to speak to me. She told Gary that I was out of pocket for what I had done. If she felt that way I was cool with it. I wish she would have come out of her mouth and told me. We hadn't never had a third party to transfer messages before and I wasn't going to start. Shit had been going on for way to long now. It was time for her to come back. I needed her to help me make my next move. I went as far as calling her Uncle Stacey to get him to talk to her. That was something I never did. I was a grown man it made me feel less of man to have to go to him. The only advice he could give me was to let her come back on her own terms. I needed her more than ever. I need to figure out how we were going to bounce back from this.

I wish I could discuss this with Lourdes but she ended up being called out of the country. Something was going on with her family. I was relieved that she didn't get caught up in the drama. I don't know what I would do if something happened to her. I promised myself when things died down I was going to tell her everything. There was no use to continue taking things forward if I couldn't keep it a hundred with her. I decided to tell her the truth about me when she returned. If she could accept all of me then I would go ahead and pop the question. I know it seemed soon, but she was the one for me. I couldn't see myself with anyone else.

***

Later on that evening I decided to take a ride to the center to check on the makeshift shelter. This was the first time I had been in the city since the bombings. The place looked like a war zone. The National Guard was posted on every corner. There was still an ash gray cloud hovering over the city; it reeked of burnt carnage. I drove into the river front and pulled into my parking lot.

There was a Christiana Care mobile medical center on the premises.

Several food trucks and unmarked police cars including a FEMA vehicle. Raela had did her thing to make sure we looked like saints. I knew I could count on her to put us in the clear. I smiled as I walked towards the building. Once I was at the door I slid my card into the electronic pad to gain entrance.

The office area was deserted. I walked through the hallway and entered into the main lobby. I was greeted by straight action. There was tables lines up with pampers, formula. Donated clothes, blankets anything you needed in the time of an emergency. My heart softened because despite my actions I was still there to help my community. I could only imagine how they would feel if they knew I was the one who caused there lost.

As soon as I walked through I was met by a news reporter from the New Journal. I told her I would have our spokesperson put together a statement for them. I didn't feel right speaking about it.

After a few brief conversations I made it to the gym. There had to be about forty families residing there. There were hospital curtains sectioning off areas giving everyone a lil privacy. I lowered my head. *Man I can't have these people living like this.*

"Dorian!" I turned in the direction of the voice. It was Queen she was over in the corner in what seemed to be makeshift daycare. I walked over to her and hugged her. Her eyes shifted from me to the occupants.

"Ne-Ne, come over here and sit with this kids for a minute." She called out to a young intern that worked in the children's department.

"Let's go to your office we need to talk." She was stern. I followed behind her like a little boy who was about to be scolded. I didn't say anything as we walked down the hallway.

We arrived at my office. We went inside, she locked the door. My heart dropped and I felt anxious. I had no idea why. It wasn't like she was about to whoop my ass. I was too damn old for that. I couldn't change how I felt though. I sat down in my leather chair she sat in front of me.

There was a brief moment of silence before she spoke.

"Dorian, when I chose you to take my place. I had big plans for you. I chose you because you were the only one I knew who would have the heart to carry out what needed to be done. I heard about the competition, I want you to know I agree with you from shutting them down.

However, there is a way to do everything. You have done more harm than good. I wish you would have consulted with me or at least Stacey before you went this far. This is a national disaster, baby. Nothing good is going to come from this. I hate to say it's only a matter of time before somehow they connect this shit to the family." To my surprise Queen spoke calm but there was weariness on her face. "Baby, maybe we should leave this alone.

Let Raela focus on building the enterprise legally and jump on board with Gary and this music thing. Careem is really good. I believe he can go far." She spoke with optimism. If I wasn't sitting dead in her face I would have sworn I was talking to some square old broad. She wasn't-the almighty ride or die, get down own get ran the fuck over; Queen was sitting in my presence talking some sucker shit.

"I guess Gary got to you too," I turned my head and played with my dreads. I couldn't look at her in her face. This was not the same merciless woman who turned me on to the game so many years ago.

She reached for my hand. "Baby, this is not worth it. We have more than enough. Did you ever think about what we stand to lose if you get caught up in this? All of the hard work, all of the street work will be in vain. Dorian, everything I did in these streets was to make a better life for my kids."

I heard everything she was saying but I couldn't believe it was coming out of her mouth. Things were hectic-yes. However, she and everyone else had to realize I was raised this way. She was the main one who had instilled the importance of maintaining control in these streets. We never were the type to strong hand a nigga. It wasn't until we were crossed that I had to force my hand. They brought this on themselves.

CHAPTER EIGHTEEN

Today I was meeting with Lourdes for the first time in weeks. I had offered to pick her up from the airport-she declined. Instead I met her at the Parking lot of University of Delaware's Bob Carpenter Center. I didn't know what that was all about we could have went to her Condo or she could have even chilled at my crib. It was about time for her to meet my kids anyway. I pulled into the parking lot and spotted the navy blue state issued Chevy Malibu she was driving. *She must be working.* I hadn't even thought about that. Maybe this was the reason she didn't want to come to the house. I parked next to her and unlocked her door. She opened her door and walked over to the passenger side of my vehicle. There was something different about her she seemed to move slower and she looked worn out. She opened it and got in.

I greeted her with a kiss. She cut it short by pulling away in haste. "Damn is that how you do me after damn near three weeks of being apart?" I gave a hint of a laugh but I really was hot. I had too much going on for my baby to act weak with me too. She leaned her head back on the headrest her neck lazily turned in my direction. There was no expression on her face. Her eyes were dull and her face was sunken in. I looked her up and down and she seemed to have lost weight.

"Lourdes, you good?"

"No-not really, that's the reason why I called you here. Dorian, I have so much going on right now. The events that took place in Wilmington have the Government in an uproar. I will be spending a lot of time between Washington and Dover.

Then there is my family back home. I have to get things in order with them. I don't know when I will have time to be with you. I'm tired mentally and physically. I don't think it's fair to have you hanging on when I have no idea when I will have time to build a relationship with you." Her eyes weld with tears.

I felt a knot in the pit of my stomach. This is the first time I regretted bombing the city. I didn't think about how it would effect Lourdes position in the government. The thing is Gary and Queen was right, I didn't think period. I only saw minuses in front of dollar signs. I refused to lose Lourdes, I was going to do whatever it took for us to make this relationship work.

I took her hand and kissed it.

"Lourdes, I never met a woman quite like you. You give me sunlight on my darkest days, you quench my thirst, and you are my rib. Together we can conquer the world. I can't see myself being with out you. That's why I have to make you my wife."

Lourdes head dropped and she burst into tears. I wiped her tears away gently and kissed her face. "Baby, don't cry we are going to be alright. I promise to take care of you for the rest of my life." I pulled her into my chest as she sobbed.

"I-I want to be your wife but I have too much going on in my life. You wouldn't understand. I can't be the wife you deserve." She starred in my eyes sincerely.

"You don't have to be perfect. I'm not perfect and we can work this out-together. I will not accept a no!" I grabbed on to her arms firmly.

"I have to leave for Washington tonight for a week or so. I want you to come with me. We can stay at one of the hotels at the National Harbor. That way I will be in close proximity to the Capital. We can discuss it then. There is so much I need to tell you about me, then you can make the decision if you want me to be Mrs. Dorian Reynolds."

CHAPTER NINETEEN

Lourdes and I ended up staying at the Gaylord National Resort at the Harbor. She insisted that we talked but I had other things in mind. I had so much stress and I was backed up. The only thing on my mind was getting up inside of her. I lay her gently on the bed and undressed her slowly. I kissed and sucked on her exposed body parts. I slid my tool into her tight hole. For some reason she seemed extra moist-I loved it. I stroked her until we both passed out in each other's arms.

The next morning she had to be in Washington bright and early. She left before I woke up. She left me a sweet note telling me she wouldn't be back until after seven. She had to attend a dinner meeting. I knew that she was going to be busy. I didn't mind as long as I could spend every free moment with her. I got up and showered. I would call the office to let them know I would be back next week after breakfast. I turned my phone off because I didn't want any interruptions while I was planning life with my future wife.

I called room service and ordered a Mimosa, Western Omelets and a side of hash browns. This wasn't my normal morning regimen; I was on vacation I was going to enjoy myself. Twenty minutes my breakfast was served. I lay back in the bed in my boxers and enjoyed my food. I refused to let anything bother me. I turned the television on an ordered a movie. I wanted to see something funny. With all the tragic shit going on in my life; I needed something to lighten things up. I ended up falling asleep; I woke up to a blue screen. I picked up my watch off the table to check the time. It was well after three in the afternoon. *Damn I really needed that rest.*

I got up and went to the bathroom. I looked out the window and noticed for the first time how bright the sun was shining. I decided to get dress and do a little shopping. I saw a FOSSIL store when we drove in last night. I wanted to get her a nice watch or purse.

Shit I probably would get her both. What I really should be shopping for was a ring. I was going to the Tiffany Store this weekend. I had it all planned I was going to have Queen prepare dinner at my house and then propose to her in front of the kids. I was going to have to talk to Darriana maybe even throw a car in the mix. She couldn't see me with any woman ever.

I grabbed my phone and the room key card and left out.

***

I ended up buying two Fossil bags a burnt orange and teal. I noticed that Lourdes wore colors that would coincide well with them. I went to South Moon Under to get few outfits for my daughters they would have a heart attack if I came back empty handed. It was bad enough no one knew where my ass was in the first place. I planned to turn my phone on when I got back to the room, I declared today a me day and I was going to enjoy it.

I shopped until the sun hid beyond the Horizon. I had so many bags I could feel the blood circulation cutting off from my fingers. I didn't know how broads did it. Shopping should be considered a sport. Colleges would be full if broads could get a scholarship for shopping skills. I laughed to myself at the thought. *That would be some shit.*

I was hungry as a mother fucker but decided to skip out on going to a restaurant; I was tired and these bags had to be dropped off. I went straight to my room when I opened the door I heard soft music playing, it was Lauryn Hill crooning the *Sweetest Thing*. That was my shit.

I dropped the bags at the door and went towards the bedroom. Lourdes dark chocolate body was laying upon a bed of pale pink rose petals. If I was a photographer I would have snapped her picture. That was definitely a money shot. She was sexy in an artistic type way. People would pay top dollar for such a display of beauty. *Damn I love this broad.* I walked to the bed and sat on the edge of it. I spread her thick thighs and planted kisses on the inner parts until I made my way to her treasure. I leaned back for a moment and starred at the perfect plump lips and the thick pink clit slightly peeked out, I licked my lips and removed my coat. I threw it to the floor and my phone fell out. I series of chimes rang out back to back which caught my attention. I didn't turn my phone on.

The button was sensitive; it must have turned its self on when it hit the floor. The phone was still going off. Although I didn't want to I was too curious not to look at it to see who was sending me all of these messages and why. I picked it up and there was seventy missed text messages from Queen and Gary. My voicemail was full as well. I read through the messages and they were all saying something happened and I needed to call home immediately. I knew it had to be serious if they didn't say what the issue was on a text. I called Gary immediately. He answered on the first ring.

"*Nigga, why the fuck ain't you answering the phone!*"

"I'm away on vacation. Why y'all blowing my shit up like that. What's up?"

"Vacation?" Gary huffed. "Mother fucker why you out vacationing your little sister went missing. Them mother fuckas we hit kidnapped her. They talking bout they want a million in ransom to get her back!"

I jumped from the bed and paced back and forth. My head was pounding and my heart felt like it was about to fall to my stomach.

"Who they got Mish or Bree?"

"*Izzo, they snatched Bree up from school!*"

"How the fuck they know what school she went to? How they know she was our sister? Shit how the fuck they know it was us-unless we got a snitch!"

"*Right! Queen losing her mind we thought we was going to have to take her to the hospital last night. Her pressure shot up high as shit. Dutch and Careem is out now trying to find answers.*"

"Careem? Why the fuck ain't he in school? Why is he with Dutch?"

I didn't want Careem involved in this shit he had too much going for him. He did not need to be involved in the street life for real.

"Nigga, just get back home and I will fill you in on everything and I ain't talking about this shit over no jack." He hung up.

I picked up my coat and put it back on in a hurry. Lourdes was sitting up in the bed registering every thing that took place.

"Dorian, is everything ok?" she whispered.

"Naw, shit got real. Fucking with my money is one thing but my family-mother fuckas is asking to visit dirt."

Lourdes slid from the bed and ran over to me. There was a look of surprise and confusion on her face. "Dorian, you are scaring me. I never heard you talk this way before. What is happening? Who took your sister? Why would they want to take your sister?" she reached out to touch me and I moved away. A tear dropped from her eye.

"Look babe, I'm sorry but I got to go. There is another side to me that I don't think you're ready for. I'm not sure how things are going to turn out. I need you to stay far way from me until shit is safe. I couldn't bare to see anything happen to you on the count of my beef.

Lourdes shook her head, "Dorian, I fear no man or woman on this earth. I can handle anything and I refuse to lose you! I won't lose you-I can't" she pounded her fist into my chest. I kissed her lips and left out the door without looking back.

CHAPTER TWENTY

Lourdes

I ran to the door and pulled it open. "Dorian, I need to tell you something!" I shouted at the top of my lungs. The elevator doors opened and he got on keeping his back turned towards me. I ran completely naked to the elevator as fast as I could. I refused to let him leave without telling him everything about me. The doors closed before I could stop it.

"No!" I cried out. I fell to the floor in a fetal position and cried. This can't be happening. I loved this man with all of my heart. I would do anything to be with him.

I felt a faint touch on the shoulder an older white woman was standing before me. "Dear do you need me to call someone for you?"

I looked down at my exposed breast and Vagina.

"Thank, you I'm fine. I'm sorry." I got up and ran to my room. I didn't need anyone recognizing me. This was D.C and for all I know I may sit at the table with her husband discussing politics.

When I reached the room I pulled my cell from the drawer. I spoke the words, *Chez Moi.* I was connected to my home in St. Lucia

"*Bonsior*"

"Bonsior, Gazelle." I greeted my second sister.

"*Comment-allez-vous?*""That all depends on the answers you give me..."*"Why is that sister?*" Gazelle could speak perfect English but preferred to speak French. She hated the Americans ways.

"Do we have a girl-a young girl captive by chance?"

"*No-should we?*"

I took a deep breath relieved that we had nothing to do with the kidnapping; however, I still had an odd feeling about everything.

"Did we have any leads on who sabotaged the houses here?"

"*Actually, we do have a lead,*" I could here the smile in her voice. "*There is a man called-The Street President. His family is supposed to run the streets in Wilmington and the East coast. We found his wife in Miami.*"

"A wife, that's wonderful!" I could breathe again it wasn't Dorian. I was going to be his wife. "Send Sosa, and Xavier for her. I want them to make her suffer. Don't kill her right away; she needs to be vegetated so he can see he fucked with the wrong family. After the wife, kill off the rest of his kin. I lost my nephews because of him and you lost your only children. He will suffer greatly for it!"

She fell silent.

"*So be it...Salute.*"

"Salute." I then disconnected the call.

CHAPTER TWENTY-ONE

I arrived at Queens's house and everyone was there including Dutch and Careem. When I walked in the room the gloom overtook me. Queen was on the couch laying there staring into space. My eyes stung and I could feel the tears coming. I couldn't let them flow though. I had to stay strong.

Dutch pulled me to the side. "Yo, come out back with me real quick I got show you something." I nodded and followed behind him. Careem was right on my tracks. When he got on the porch I turned to him. "Reem, stay out of this shit. You got good shit going, this ain't your life."

"Big bro, with all respect you can save that shit. Bree is like my twin. I'm connected to her more than I am with any of y'all. Bree is hard headed but she's my heart. You have to respect that!" I never seen that look on his face in my life. Careem was usually the cocky jokester, not today. He had the demeanor of a bonafide killer. He was passionate about his mission, I couldn't stop him no matter how I felt about it. I said no more and followed Dutch around back.

Queen had a small shed out back that was used for storage. Dutch unlocked it and opened the door. I was greeted by a pungent odor.

"What the fuck!"

I covered my nose and mouth and stepped in. It was dark so I used the flashlight on my key ring to see. There was a naked female tied to the post covered in dark red blood from the waist down. There were gaping wounds on her thighs and legs. I moved the flashlight down and noticed chunks of flesh at her feet. I had to keep the vomit from spewing from my mouth.

"Who-man what the fuck is going on?" I started to gag.

Dutch laughed, "Nigga, don't tell me you getting soft on a nigga. I remember back in the day we used to gut niggas on a regular. Now you on some throwing up shit like a bitch-you ain't cut out for this no more, Izzo."

"Fuck outta here nigga, don't ever question my goon status. You just caught a nigga off guard. I wasn't ready for this shit, now what the fuck is really going on!" This nigga was irritating me. Our sister was missing he wanted to play Edward Scissor hands.

"What's going on is this bitch know where Bree at. We going to get her tonight. This ho going to lead us right to her, Ain't you cutie." Dutch licked his lips and the girl nodded her head. I moved the flashlight closer in on the girl. She didn't look no older than my daughter Ariel, she was a kid.

"Yo, this is a little girl how she gone do that?"

"Little girl? Nigga she suck a dick like ho in her forties. This youngin right here is your ole crazy bitch niece. You know the Santa Bitch- What's her name?"

"TaNeka?"

"Yup, that crazy ass ho…They used this lil bitch to bait Bree in. They go to the same school. This dumb bitch been collecting Bree's assignments and turning them in. I sent Reem in to the school to talk to a few people to see what they knew. They said, the last time they seen Bree was when she left with old Kimmie here. So I sent pretty boy Floyd in to run game on her…"

"You know the bitches can't resist me," Careem interrupted. "I got the bitch to top me off before I told her I was Cabree brother. I beat the shit out of her and after I searched the car I found several copies of the ransom note. The bitch so stupid she had to practice writing the fucking note, and kept the evidence." For a minute I thought it was Dutch talking, Reem had picked up his ways.

I leaned back on the wall. This TaNeka Bitch was out of control. I couldn't believe she would go this far. Broads like her needed to be expired. She wasn't safe to society.

"Did you tell mom?" I asked Dutch.

"Naw, nobody knows she is here besides us. I want to get this bitch outta of here and bring Bree home safe to Queen. If something went wrong, I don't want her to have her hopes up."

I felt that. You never know what could happen when you go to war.

***

Careem and Dutch wrapped Kimmies bottom half up tightly in plastic. They made her call home to let her people's know that she was on her way home. We drove out to the Lexington Green. When we got out there she told us that they were keeping her in an abandoned apartment in the Village of Windover. We went over there but I got out the car and walked to the address she gave on stone place.

I wanted to make sure everything was legit. I went around the back of the apartment that was located on the first floor and stood next to the sliding glass door. I heard movement and could see the flashing of the television in the darkness. I heard a knock at the door.

"Who is it! "It was TaNeka's voice I heard. "Why ain't that bitch use her key? I heard her complain. I heard a few male voices too. I knew there was ready to be a problem. I had to think fast. Kimmie couldn't walk so one of them was carrying her. I pressed my ear against the glass door, I made sure my safety was off the AK. As soon as I heard the words, "Oh shit!" I blasted through the glass door dumping rounds. I aired the two niggas out on the spot.

"Oh my GOD Prez, I swear they made me do it!" TaNeka screamed. Her scream was cut short when a bullet from the Desert E, Careem was carrying penetrated her skull.

Dutch dumped Kimmies body on the ground and Careem aimed his gun to her head, "Where the fuck is my sister bitch!"

She pointed to the back, "Please don't kill me." She begged. Careem and Dutch ran to the back and found Cabree naked on the bed drugged up. Careem ran out the room. "What the fuck you do to my sister!" He punched her in the face repeatedly. I grabbed him.

"We got to go, it's hot out here!" With tears running down his face. He let of the shots one to each eye then her mouth. Dutch grabbed everything that belonged to Cabree wrapped her up in sheets and we fled the scene.

CHAPTER TWENTY-TWO

We found out that the dudes in the house had taken turns raping Cabree. They were Kimmie's cousins. They had been forcing her to take Xanax, and Ambien which could have been deadly.

Queen was so hurt to see her baby in that condition. We couldn't take her to the hospital in Delaware it would be too many questions asked. Gary drove her to Chester and left her at a bus stop closest to Crozier hospital. We had Misha go with her to watch her and make sure things went as planned. Forty-five minutes later we received a phone call from the Chester police stating our sister was there.

We drove up there and everyone played their part. The cops interviewed Queen, she told them she was staying with a best friend for a few days. We never knew there was a problem. Dutch left and cleaned up the shed. He knew how to clean a scene. If he ever wanted to do right that nigga could have been apart of a CSI team.

Careem was shaken up. It had just hit him that he had killed two people. He would never be the same and I wasn't sure if that was a good or bad thing. I called our family in Atlanta and told them he needed to be there for a while. Dutch would fill them in on everything once they got there.

The next morning Queen said her good-byes to Careem and he headed down south until we could sort all this mess out.

They released Cabree from the hospital the next afternoon. Gary went to get her with Queen. I was sitting in her living room when they returned.

"How you feel Bree?" I went over to hug her and she pushed me away with the little strength she had.

"Fuck you, Prez. How do you think I feel? They raped me? TaNeka made them rape me and she taped it. It's all over you tube!" she busted out crying. "I fuckin' hate you!"

It felt like a sword went straight through my heart. I couldn't help it. The tears fell. I broke down and fell back on the chair like a bitch. This was all my fault. My sister was violated and it was broadcasted on the World Wide Web.

I felt a hand rubbing my back. "Son, it's ok. She didn't mean it. She's hurt right now. The police is going to make sure that shit is off the web. The people responsible are gone."

"Mom, I didn't mean for this to happen. I love Bree, she's like my daughter. I feel like someone raped Ariel or Darianna. There's still one more person that needs to be got. That's Kimmie's mom, TaNeka sister. She going to go to the police. This ain't over."

"Oh but it is over. Dutch took care of her last night. He knew she would go to check out the scene. She never made it out of her apartment."

"I need to talk to Raela. I need my friend right now." Life was too short for the bullshit beef we were having. I needed her more than ever. She was the only one who could help me make sense of things.

"Her plane arrived twenty minutes ago." She called me last night. She had important news to tell you concerning the connect for the crystal shit. I told her about Bree and she booked the first flight out." Gary walked in to the living room. "She couldn't get a flight into Philly so she had to fly into BWI. I would have picked her up but she insisted I stayed with the family."

With everything going on that crystal shit was the last thing on my mind. I didn't even care about it anymore. If a crazy bitch would go as far as kidnapping, raping and drugging my teenage sister because I took the dick away from her. Ain't no telling what these mother fuckers would do if they found out we were the ones who fucked there operation up. I was done with this shit.

When Raela came, I was going to let her know I am going legit. Lourdes came to my mind. I felt like shit for leaving her the way that I did. I was going to make it right. I stood up and put on my coat. I still had time to make it to Tiffany's- I had a ring to buy.

CHAPTER TWENTY-THREE

I purchased a 2.5 platinum three stone emerald cut engagement ring from Tiffany's. It wasn't exactly what I wanted but it would do for now. I called Lourdes while I was on the highway back to Queens. I apologized and let her know that I had my sister back. She didn't ask a bunch of questions. She stated she was just happy to hear my voice. She told me that she was going to drive back to Delaware in the morning. She had a business meeting in early in the day but we could meet at her Condo to discuss our marriage.

To hear that word come out of her mouth lifted heaviness that was on me for years. I was finally going to settle down and do the normal thing; It wasn't until that moment did I realize that's all I wanted all along was to chill and be happy.

Tomorrow my life was changing for the better.

CHAPTER TWENTY-FOUR

At three o'clock in the morning I woke up to a loud, "NOOOOO!!!!" I sat up on the couch and Gary was on his cell phone cursing and yelling. Queen ran down the stairs and I tried to adjust my senses so I could understand what the hell was going on.

I thought Gary had been left. We were waiting for Raela to show up from the airport. Hours went by and she never showed. Gary called the airport to make sure that she arrived. He even tried to have the rental car located, but that wasn't happening. The last thing I remembered was Gary saying he was going home to check in with Erica so she wouldn't snap.

"Gary what's wrong!" Queen wrapped her robe around herself. When he didn't answer she snatched his phone, "Hello, my son is too upset to talk can you tell me what's going on?" she said.

Whatever was said on the other end wasn't good, Queens knees buckled. I jumped to catch her before she hit the floor. "God no, Oh God no!" she cried.

Gary ran out the house and I heard him peel off in his truck.

"Mom what's going on?" I needed answers. I wasn't sure if something happened to Careem or Dutch.

"We got to go to Christina hospital now! It's Raela she not gonna make it!"

"What-what do you mean! What happened Queen! What the fuck happened to Raela!" Spit spewed from my mouth, it felt like I had bricks in my throat. I didn't understand what the fuck was going on. Queen ran upstairs and threw on something and we rushed to the hospital. So many thought were going through my mind. Was she in a car accident? Did Marco's family retaliate? I had been trying to contact her Uncle Stacey all day and there was no answer.

We arrived to the hospital and went to the information desk. We let them know we were family and they sent us to her unit. There was a state trooper outside the door watching the doctor talk to Gary who was broken up badly. I never really knew that Gary and Raela was that close for him to be acting the way he was. Her and Dutch spent more time together than they did. I walked up on the conversation in time to hear the doctor explaining her condition, "She is "brain dead" she suffered tremendous damage to her brain when she was attacked. She is being kept alive with the help of a ventilator that is aiding her breathing, her heart will still beat, her skin color will remain the same, everything will function normally;

which means the child can grow and be nourished until we can perform a safe caesarean birth.

I had her medical records sent to me and she has a Dorian Reynolds as her Health directive and Gary Reynolds is listed as the child she is carryings father?" He raised his eyebrow. Gary nodded his head. I looked at Queen and she didn't seem to be surprised at the news of Raela being pregnant at all. No wonder Gary was going off. He was fucking Raela the whole time. I felt betrayed and didn't know why. She wasn't my girl. But why didn't they tell me.

"How did this happen? What happened?"

"A family found her body lying outside the car on I-95 a few hours go. She was beaten with a steel object in her head. We found several small shards of metal impacted in her skull. We operated to repair what we could. Her head is enlarged from the swelling. It will eventually go down.

Right now she will probably not look anything of how you remembered her. The baby is doing fine she is twenty-nine weeks. We would like to keep her on the life support at least until the baby's lungs are developed enough to survive on its own. I'm so sorry for what you're going through. I have a daughter around her age. I don't understand who would want to do this to such a beautiful girl." He patted me on the shoulder and walked off.

I went into the room and there was a million tubes running throughout her body. The breathing machine was on the side of the bed doing its job. I glanced at her face and quickly turned my heard. The bandages around her head were wrapped tightly.

Her face was so big that her eyes looked like they were going to pop out. I touched her arm. It was tight and shiny but warm. I looked at the hump in under the blanket. She was pregnant. She was carrying my niece or nephew. My heart hurt; to know it was Gary's baby and not mine. I was so confused right now. I guess I never wanted to admit the feelings I had hidden for her. I had lost my best friend and my brother would always have apart of her. I was envious of him at the moment.

"What is Erica going say about your new baby?" I snapped. Gary was shaking. "Fuck Erica, I filed for divorce. When Careem and I went down for his show.

Raela and I brought a crib. I was going to marry her and now a mother fucker took her away from me and I want to know why! My child is going to grow up with out her mother! I swear on her life, that whoever responsible for this shit is going to die! I promise you!" He broke out in tears. I went over and hugged him. We cried together. We both loved her in our own way and he was right whoever did this was going to die!

All Good things must come to an end…

Lourdes…

"Yes, Sosa."

"*I left an envelope at the consuiers desk for you. It's finished.*"

"Merci, Sosa." *Let the games begin.* I slipped on my shoes and headed to the first floor to take a look at my victim's wife.

Christina Hospital…

Misha came to pick Queen up. She refused to visit Raela. She said she wanted to remember her the way she knew her. I understood that. I called Amber, and the rest of the family. Everyone was broken up over it. Darianna demanded to come see her. She and Lil Dorian were very close to her. Amber was going to bring her after school. I tried to contact Dutch but his phone was off. I called Stacey again and still couldn't contact him. That was beginning to worry me. Gary had a bad feeling too. It wasn't like him not to call back. I was going to tell Lourdes about Raela when we met up later. I know she didn't get down with her like that, but she knew my feelings for her. An hour past and I was starting to get hungry.

Gary refused to leave Raela's side. I think he had it in his mind that she was going to wake up. I wish she would also-God knows I did. I went down the grill to get us some fries and burgers. I placed my order and sat down at the table to wait for the food to be done.

As I was waiting my phone chirped. I had a text message. I opened it up it was from Dutch, a picture of Stacey's dead body was attached. My jaw dropped. Two more pictures came through they were documents-deeds. Copies of the deeds to the Apple street properties from L&G Properties on the Deed the names Lourdes and Gizelle Laveau. *It can't be, no it she can't be!* My soul left my body after seeing that. My phone rang. It was Dutch.

"Izzo, Imma merk that bitch! Mommy told me what happened to Raela. Why is it that all the bitches you fuck with fucks us over! Why can't you fuck with some ole' hoodrat bitch? Your Senator bitch is running a major fucking drug ring. There is no connect for that crystal shit because her family manufactures it in St. Lucia. One of her sisters was killed by the Haitians because they were stepping on their territory. The bitch hand reaches far, and they are vicious."

"How you find all this out?" I walked to the parking lot to my car. Tears were running down my face. I couldn't believe what I was hearing this bitch played me from the beginning.

"I called Stacey to tell him I was going to come chill with him for a minute to clear my mind after all the Careem and Bree shit.

He told me to come on because he wanted to rap to me about some serious shit. I get down there at like five this morning. And this nigga is slumped over in the chair with a bullet to the brain. I went to Raela's, because you know I got key to check her out and she is gone.

I find all these documents on her desk with your bitch name on it. Raela must have hired a private investigator. There are pictures of you with this bitch, Pictures of the bitch at the scene of the explosions, and going in and out of other trap houses. Nigga she the fucking God Mother of the Cartel you been sleeping with the fucking enemy all this time. I know you love this bitch. Once Gary finds out it's a rap. Either you do the honors or I will. The choice is yours." The phone went dead.

Lourdes...

"My God no..." I held the pictures of Raela's beaten body in my shaking hand. "How could this be? This makes no sense. She's not married to Prez. Dorian would have told me. I went to the next picture and it sickened me. She was pregnant. "Oh God, I held my own stomach." I was no friend of hers but the fact that I had my future husband business partner and best friend killed made me ill. I should have told him everything from the beginning. Maybe he would have told me about Raela and her husband and we could have worked something out. It seems as history was repeating itself; when the Haitians killed my sister, Aralles two years ago. I promised to do things differently. Gizelle and her thick head wanted to run things the same and by doing that her sons were killed. *I should have followed my instincts and kept it down south.* It was too late now.

I washed my face and took a valium. Dorian was soon to come and I had to prepare myself for the worse. I knew he needed me now more than ever. I tossed the envelope into my fireplace I couldn't bare to see her in that state.

My doorbell rang. I took a deep breath and buzzed him in.

Dorian...

I rode the elevator to her floor. Once the doors open I pulled my gun from the back of my pants and removed the safety. I turned the knob and opened the door. Lourdes was sitting in a black silk robe drinking a glass of merlot with a blameless expression on her face. "Hey baby, how are you?" she stood up slowly. I locked the door behind me and stared at her. How could she act like nothing happened after what she just did? I kept my hand behind my back and walked toward her slowly. She had a dazed look in her eyes. Something wasn't right with her.

"Dorian, are you okay?" She stopped and looked at my arm. "What's behind your back Dorian?" her tone was shaky. There it was she was guilty. I pulled Tiffany box from my left pocket. A smile went on her face and she grabbed her chest. I flipped it open so she could see the ring.

"Oh my God it's breath taking. Oh, thank God I thought you were upset."

"Why would I be upset, Lourdes?"

"I mean the way you were looking. I thought something might have happened-I don't know. But I love it. Are you going to place it on my finger?" She held her hand out to me.

"Yeah," I placed the box on the table and revealed my right hand holding the gun. She gasped and backed up. "I have a few questions first."

She held her chest and began to breathe heavy, "Dorian, please let me explain. I didn't know it was Raela. They told me they found the guy's Prez's wife and I gave them the go ahead to do what needed to be done. I never knew it was Raela. I thought she only worked for you. You never mentioned that she was married. I tried to tell you about who I was in Washington but your sister was kidnapped, then my family's business was almost destroyed by that Prez guys. My nephews were killed in that explosion. It was just too much. Then you popped marriage on me. It seemed like it was never the right time to tell you."

"What the fuck are you talking about? Raela is not married to Prez! I'm Prez! Raela was engaged to my brother. She was carrying his baby now she is a vegetable only being kept alive so that my niece or nephew she is carrying can survive!"

"You're Prez?" she tilted her head to the side. "How can that be? I know everything about you. You aren't in the streets."

"Just like I thought I knew everything about you. I guess we were both wrong. I love you Lourdes, but I can't let you live. Not after this. I can't..." I cocked the gun. Her eyes got big and she reached in the pocket of her robe. "Wait!"

I pulled the trigger and her body jolted to the floor. I walked over to her body and there was a pool of blood leaking from her body. I reached in her pocket to retrieve her gun. Instead of a gun there was a picture. I pulled it out and looked at it. It was an ultra sound. Lourdes was thirteen weeks pregnant...

To be continued...

CASH TALKS PUBLISHING GROUP

www.ingramcontent.com/pod-product-compliance
Lightning Source LLC
Chambersburg PA
CBHW060116260626
47160CB00005B/1903